# BODY AND SOUL

# BODY AND SOUL

J. P. Smith

THOMAS & MERCER

The characters and events portrayed in this book are fictitious. Any similarity to real persons, living or dead, is coincidental and not intended by the author.


Printed in the United States of America.


Published by Thomas & Mercer
P.O. Box 400818
Las Vegas, NV 89140

ISBN-13: 9781612185682
ISBN-10: 1612185681

*For Cheryl*

# 1

FIVE NIGHTS A WEEK JERZY WOZZECK PLAYED THE PIANO at a quiet little bistro on the Boulevard Saint Michel. He played two sets an evening, from seven-thirty until nine and from half-past nine till eleven. When he played he neither acknowledged his audience (such as it was), nor troubled to introduce his pieces, as other musicians might have done. During his break he would sip a glass of beer, smoke two cigarettes, and, as a matador sizes up his bull, stare purposefully and with faint trepidation through his dark glasses at the instrument standing on the little wooden platform. The building in which this took place was located about halfway between the Place Saint Michel and the Palais du Luxembourg, like the thin edge of a wedge keeping apart an American fast-food restaurant and a carpeted, elegantly appointed bookshop specializing in disseminating the works of the late Louis Althusser.

An establishment of shifting identities, the bistro had over the years variously advertised itself as Le Mainstream, Le Bebop, Le Jazz-Cool, Le Jazz-Hot, Le West-Coast, Le Trad, Les Autres, Le New-Wave, Le Twist, Le Disco-Cool, Le Disco-Hot, Le Pin-Ball, Le Je m'en fous, and so on, according to the trend of the moment (or rather the state of mind of its clientele, for the quality and type of music had not once been altered, though this had escaped the notice of all but a few). It was known to its habitués simply as "the club," possessing a reputation among jazz fans and musicians as the only place worth visiting if one lacked the fare to New York. It was dirty, strewn with sawdust, the beer was flat, the wine corked, its bathrooms unspeakably primitive (which for a brief time caused the club to be known as Le Trou), the air rank; yet the music was sublime and the atmosphere electric.

Journalists who profited from this genre of music (and who edited short-lived magazines called *Le Jazz-Hot*, *Le Jazz-Cool*, *Le New-Wave*, etc.) had, in its day, congregated there; agents in sharkskin suits and dark glasses, pontifically nursing cigars, sought out new talent as candidates periodically bobbed into view through the thick Havana haze, and eager young trumpeters and saxophonists sat cradling their instrument cases and munching salted peanuts in the hope that Dizzy Gillespie or John Coltrane might drop dead and leave the stand open to them. Legend even had it that on one Saturday night Miles Davis, in his surly sixties mood, had, perhaps because he was accustomed to a better class of facility, destroyed the men's convenience with a few well-placed right hooks.

It was thus something of a tragedy to Jerzy Wozzeck when the management changed. Now food was served; now it was called Le Hamburger-Hot.

"You see what they have done?" Wozzeck was complaining to his wife Heidi soon after the transformation had taken place. "They tell me, 'No bebop, Wozzeck, no new tunes, no block chords. Just tinkle your little keys like a good boy and no one will be hurt.' What can I do? If I try something different, maybe a little tune by Charlie Parker, they call me in afterward and make me sit in a corner of the office. Then they carry on a conversation among themselves, as if I were already a dead man, about what a pity it is that Monsieur So-and-so was found floating in the Seine. I don't understand these French people, they speak in riddles, like Russians."

What perhaps hurt Wozzeck most was that, although before he had played on the same platform with some of the biggest names in the business, he now performed alone. And though to be a headliner had been his greatest wish since his early days in Warsaw, he now discovered that a kind of void had been created about him. For with the ambiance also had gone the agents, the journalists, the fellow musicians with their jibes and shop talk, and thus any chance for his succeeding in a world governed by word of mouth, lucky breaks, and venality.

But most of his other émigré friends, who previously had felt uneasy in the dark uncertainty of the club, welcomed the change. Yards of linoleum and a selection of plastic tables and chairs had replaced the battered wood and little unsteady stools of a previous era. Greedy electronic amusements, sinister boxes loaded with flashing lights and sounds of war, that to the profit of organized crime tantalized and outwitted the imaginations of vacuous adolescents, were placed strategically at the entrance. Proper ceiling lamps bathed the diners in a dispiriting glow of fluorescence, while carefully aimed spotlights removed all further doubt, so that the club, no longer a den of deepening shadows and lost perspective, had shed the appearance of being a place where one could obtain an abortion, puff opium, commit murder, and, almost incidentally, listen to music. It seemed to Jerzy's friends that after a dark age of superstition and chaos had come the enlightenment, an era of mercantile realism, the birth of capitalism and democratic principles. Now it was run by Corsican gangsters.

"Wozzeck," his friends would say, "has never truly left Warsaw. Now, Heidi is a different story. You would never imagine she had been raised in Leipzig, there is nothing of the East German about her, she has learned how to live in the West. But Wozzeck is doomed to be a Pole forever."

One evening Kupki, who was also down on his luck, came to the club with a proposition for Jerzy. Wozzeck was doodling with the notes of "April in Paris" and nodded slightly when he saw him enter. Ever since their school days in Warsaw Jerzy had felt bound to Andrzej Kupki, whose melancholy disposition—this brooding intellectual quality much appreciated by the French—and a degree in philosophy hid a shrewd and scheming mind, although he had not yet been able to find an outlet for it in Paris, where it seemed someone with his qualifications was expected simply to pass his time drinking black coffee in Montparnasse cafés and tutoring indolent young scholars for their *baccalauréat*.

While waiting for his friend, Kupki smoked his pipe and watched Wozzeck at the piano. Until their arrival in Paris they had been like brothers, inseparable. Together they had roamed the streets of Warsaw, drunk beer in deserted railway sheds, picked up girls in the Old Town on Saturday nights, served as best man for each other's weddings. And even though for a time they went their separate ways—Kupki to college, Wozzeck to the music conservatory and afterward a job playing piano at the Café Constanta in Warsaw's Old Town—they had remained the best of friends. But now that Wozzeck had to a degree fulfilled his boyhood dream he had become someone quite different, having taken to wearing dark glasses indoors and out, and adopting an assortment of mannerisms and twitches which, when performing, made him look like a blind man experiencing bowel distress. "It is to make it seem as if I am suffering," Wozzeck once explained to his friend. "It is what the customers wish. If you play jazz you must act like your grandpapa was a slave."

"But your grandpapa owned the biggest delicatessen on Jerusalem Avenue," Kupki reminded him.

The pianist finished his first set and joined Kupki at the table. Someone dropped a coin into the jukebox, and a lunatic began singing: "*Tuez-moi, tuez-moi, madame, je veux mourir, mourir, mourir...*"

Wozzeck switched on his little portable cassette player and pressed the headphones against his ears. He bobbed his head to and fro as the waiter brought him a glass of beer. Kupki puffed on his pipe and returned the uneasy looks his twin reflections offered him in Wozzeck's spectacles, sinister mirrored lenses that he had lately begun wearing in place of his more traditional "shades," as he insisted on calling them.

"I got a letter from Mama today," said Kupki, reaching into his pocket and removing a wrinkled airmail envelope.

"Speak up," said Wozzeck, as at a high volume Ornette Coleman did serious damage to his eardrums.

Kupki pulled off his friend's headphones and laid them on the table. "A letter from Mama," he repeated. "She does not think she'll last the year. My Auntie Irina has had her leg amputated. Uncle Stepan—you remember him, the one with the goiter—has been running around with another woman. My sister is pregnant for the sixth time; her husband has lost his job at the foundry and is now in jail. Otherwise all is well. Mama asks to be remembered to you and Heidi, she says you should never forget that God is good."

"Yes?" said Jerzy.

"I've been thinking," said Kupki.

"Yes?"

"I need some money."

Wozzeck reached into his pocket and fished out fifty centimes.

"Not your money—I'm thinking about thousands, hundreds of thousands, millions; other people's money: the Big Time."

"Rob the Crédit Lyonnais," suggested Wozzeck. "Then they will catch you and beat you bloody and deport you back to Warsaw. There they will do you the honor of shooting you in the back of the head. Tell your mama I wish her good health and long life and may God watch over her always, even though her son is a greedy bastard who sometimes doesn't make any sense."

Kupki looked away with impatience and raked his fingers through his thick black hair. "You mean to say you're content to stay just as you are? The whole point of coming here was to take advantage of everything the West has to offer: freedom, opportunity, money—don't you want to enjoy life like all these people?" He waved his hand at the glass door beyond which young affluent Parisians, drunk on apathy, roamed the boulevard in search of novelty.

"What?" said Wozzeck. "You think I like this, that they pay me for what I do? I have to beg for every centime I earn. On Fridays I put out my hand and smile and all they do is stare at me as if I were a beggar, 'Oh, *pardon*, Wozzeck, I had forgotten this is payday. You can wait another day or two, maybe? I still have yet to go to the bank.' I was better off in Warsaw where everyone is poor and there is nothing to buy but sausages and indulgences. And you, you should talk, Philosopher, you have only Ludmilla to support. I have to help look after Heidi's mother, a notorious war criminal who I am certain shared an intimate moment with the wicked Heinrich Himmler. What is it now? Ludmilla is pregnant maybe? And whose fault is that, Philosopher, you can't blame it on history this time. I tell you, Kupki, if you need money badly, I need it worse. Heidi is going out of her mind at that cinema on the rue de la Harpe, our honeymoon has come to an end. You think she enjoys watching the same film fifty or sixty times? You think such a thing is good for a healthy mind? The part about helping people to their seats isn't bad, there's money in that, one might even consider it a charitable act at two or three francs a go. But to have to sit there day in day out staring at the same actors saying the same idiotic lines and shooting the same people is too much, especially for a beautiful and sensitive woman like Heidi. And it has begun to affect her mind, you know," he said, pressing his forefinger to his temple. "All these American films ... I tell you, Kupki, this best of all possible worlds is poison."

"And you?" asked Kupki. "You are well?"

Wozzeck gazed at him through his dark glasses. "Never been better," he said. "Very cool."

For a long time—at least since Jerzy had begun working at the club—Kupki had suspected his friend of being a drug addict and therefore slightly unbalanced, somewhat at odds with the rest of the world, for he understood that members of the jazz fraternity, besides communicating like Freemasons in a secret language, invariably took to the needle for their pleasure, and therefore passed their lives on another plane of existence. And because Kupki was naïve about such things, he pitied Wozzeck and wished he could give him counsel and a dinner of cold turkey, for an article he had read in one of his wife's French magazines suggested that such a meal led to rehabilitation and a ripe old age.

"I need money and you need money," said Kupki.

"All God's chillun need money, oh yeah."

"But the only way we're going to succeed is if we work together."

Wozzeck continued to stare at him.

"Fritzi Bindler came over today," continued Kupki. "He needs money also. So do Blotnik and Fetler. The West has let us all down, the promised land is barren, the American dream has not come true."

"We are in France, that is why the American dream has not come true."

"But they owe us something for our trouble, these people do not know what it was like eating *chlodnik* at the Praha Restaurant while the secret police in their leather coats followed you to the toilet. For years the West has been begging us to join them, they have seen the propaganda value in even one small defection, yet when we arrive we find ourselves left to drift like lost souls."

"And whose fault is that?"

"I grant you it is a shared responsibility," lectured Kupki as he applied a match to the bowl of his pipe. "But what we have failed to realize is that each of us—the émigré and the West—must go halfway; we must meet at some mutually satisfying point. We do not fully comprehend the West, while the West does not understand how we think, they do not realize we have become accustomed to a different set of rules. We have black-market minds, and they expect us to live to the fullest in a capitalist free-for-all."

Wozzeck lit a cigarette and shot the smoke from his nostrils. "You see that guy standing by the kitchen door?" With a tilt of his chin he indicated a large mustachioed man, well-tanned and wearing an expensive silk suit through which his muscles and what could only be a large automatic weapon bulged. His shirt was unbuttoned nearly to the navel, revealing an assortment of gold charms dangling from chains, medals to ward off the Evil Eye and tiny cocaine spoons. "Be cool; if he catches you staring you've had it. He's our new manager. The last one went out three weeks ago to buy some cigarettes. He never came back. Now this guy is running the place, Gino they call him. His real name is Jean-Claude, but they say if you call him that he puts his cigar up your nose. Of course the whole place is a joke, really, I don't know why I bother putting up with it. It's always the same old thing, the same old orders to follow, the same bloody routine. Soon I am sure I will have to attend a funeral. But Gino has adjusted very nicely to this brave new world, hasn't he."

"You see? Even you are fed up with it. I tell you, Jerzy, the whole world can't really be like Warsaw."

"You have a better solution?"

Kupki assumed a conspiratorial pose. "Listen," he said.

* * *

The next evening the Wozzecks celebrated their wedding anniversary. They drank vodka and shared a bottle of cheap champagne and when not dancing talked to Fetler and Blotnik and Kupki and Ludmilla and fat Bindler who played his accordian for their entertainment when Jerzy finally rose from his battered upright piano, the neighbors having twice complained of the noise.

Every half hour or so Wozzeck and Kupki would share a knowing, unamused look through the haze of cigarette smoke, and together lift their glasses in honor of some unstated future plan.

"It is a wonderful thing, marriage," Jerzy tipsily exclaimed for the third time that evening, his arm draped over Heidi's shoulder.

"We have been married—how long has it been, Jerzy?"

"Fifteen years."

"Ten," corrected Heidi.

"And I would gladly do it all over again. Certainly it hasn't been easy. We have such little money, as you know, we are in broke city, and this apartment—well, look for yourself."

Although he had often been to the Wozzecks' place, Fetler allowed his eyes to survey the living room, once again marveling over the peeling flowered wallpaper and stained linoleum, and recalling the bathroom, which swarmed with tiny brown insects that lived in colonies and thrived on old plaster. It was a place upon which the Wozzecks had not bothered to stamp their personalities, and so Fetler gazed in wonder at what he thought must be a relic of the years of the German occupation of Paris, or even the headier days of the Second Empire.

He considered also the fact that, though Wozzeck was a jazz musician and forever in the employ of misers and hoodlums, his wife had the audacity to spend all his wages on clothes and perfume, and so their apartment, which was in the grip of a general decrepitude, resembled nothing he had ever seen before, save the majority of apartments in his native Hungary. Yet Jerzy, who worshipped his wife, was content to see his money go to support Heidi's happiness; for, though she had come from a comfortable home in Leipzig, it had been widely believed among his circle in Warsaw that the East Germans were forced to live like pigs, a rumor circulated by agents of the Polish Central Committee so as to forestall any defection to that paradise on earth.

"But still we have been happy," said Heidi.

"Of course," said fat Bindler, "we all must consider ourselves fortunate to be living in the West."

"Ah, but sometimes I miss Warsaw," said Wozzeck.

"Ach, Mama even misses Leipzig," said Heidi, indicating her old mother, who, involved in her sewing, a cigarette dangling from her lower lip, in reality wished only that her daughter had instead married a man more gainfully employed, such as Hermann Prey or Dietrich Fischer-Dieskau.

"But one must consider the state of things," said Bindler. "Here we are free to go where we like, to express our opinions whatever they may be, to read the books we choose." In illustration he pulled a tattered paperback from the pocket of his jacket, a *policier*, a lurid thriller which in its original English was called *The Devil Wears a Figleaf*, and which Wozzeck had earlier lent him.

"But too much freedom can be a bad thing," said Fetler. "And that is when the authorities begin to clamp down on the people. I am told the French police have learned everything they know from Soviet textbooks."

"You are like Andrzej," said Ludmilla Kupki scornfully, "you are miserable wherever you live."

"Oh, nobody said it was going to be a bed of roses," suggested Heidi's mother, known to one and all simply as Mama, though Wozzeck had various other, more colorful names for her.

"Shut up, Berlin Betty." he said drunkenly.

"A bed of roses," said Bindler. "Surely not. Such a thing is relative."

"But let us at least be realistic," said Fetler. "Think of the terrible bureaucracy here, for instance."

"It is worse in England, believe me," said Blotnik, who had lived in Belsize Park for twenty years before fleeing to Paris. "With all their ministries and socialized medicine they are still eating the same baked beans and mashed potatoes they were enjoying, what, forty, fifty years ago."

"Ah, but remember how it was in Poland," said Kupki, glancing at Wozzeck. "I could think of worse things than beans and potatoes."

"But see how things have changed back in your motherland," said Fetler.

"Be sensible," counseled Bindler with his index finger.

"Just open your eyes and look!" cried Wozzeck. "The workers have more power than ever. People have begun to listen to one another. They make movies, they write books—even the Pope comes and goes as he pleases, as if he were walking from one room to another. A little more of that and you'll soon see me packing my bags and heading for home," he added hopelessly.

Bindler scowled and snorted. "Young people," he said, shaking his head.

"You and your pessimism," complained Kupki, passing his hand through the air and puffing furiously on his pipe. But, like Jerzy, he knew very well that all hope for their motherland had disappeared years earlier. The dreams of a people, not so long ago openly voiced, paraded through the streets, printed on broadsides, and displayed in the world's headlines, had once again become submerged in their silent prayers, to be heard only by the Savior they hoped was listening, the Savior whose betrayal and redemption was foremost in their minds.

How well Wozzeck remembered Warsaw, how easily it would rise up in his mind in all its monochrome detail.... Those gray wintry streets, the gritty windblown snow gathering in drifts on the pavements of the Old Town, cheerless faces behind steamy restaurant windows, turning toward you, turning away from fear of what you might be, and to whom you might report.... A gray world punctuated by shifting eyes and sudden glances, the thin sympathetic smile of a friend, the pursed lips of a stranger....

Wozzeck had always suspected they kept a file on him, these men of the secret police; they were fed by informers who lingered over their beer at the Café Constanta. "Wozzeck played a decadent chord this evening," he imagined they reported. "Wozzeck spoke briefly to a student activist." They kept files on all the musicians, all the students.

To play such corrupt music, to soar beyond the rules laid down by Rimsky-Korsakov and Glenn Miller, was to ask for big trouble, it was an insult to the state, a pustule on the immaculate face of socialist reality.

But where else could one go but the Constanta? It was where he and Kupki spent their afternoons, where Ludmilla would meet them after work, where eventually Heidi—whom Jerzy had met when she had come to Poland on vacation, of all things—would join them for a drink and conversation and to play the game of Find the Secret Policemen, men who stood out because they were older than anyone else there, wore suits, and left their smiles at home. In any case it was the informers you had to watch out for, they looked just like your best friends, you had to watch your step every minute of the day. And of course the moment you suspected you were being watched you began to plan your defense, it was all part of the game. And once you'd worked out your defense you quite naturally felt guilty of something, this too was one of the rules, and once you felt guilty you were as good as guilty, they could pick you up at any time, you would sweat during your interrogation, you would admit to anything.

Oh, certainly there had been happy times, those funny unforgettable moments when Mama and Papa waltzed around the living room, laughing and pretending they were in Paris, little knowing that Papa would disappear two years later, in fifty-five it was, "I'm just stepping out for a moment," he had said one evening, "there's a man here who wants to speak to me," and then he was gone, two weeks after Jerzy had turned eight.

He remembered being dragged to some ministry by Mama, being sent on to this office and that, "Where is my husband?" she would ask, and then they were off down another corridor to another office, and still another where she would state Papa's name and speak of his secure job at the printing works, his loyalty to his work, and how much all the men liked him, he had so many friends there. "We will look into it," they would say, and they were probably still looking into it thirty years later, the gears of Polish bureaucracy are slow and rusted, they cannot keep up with the heartbeat of a grieving wife.

Sometimes, when he came of age, Jerzy would go himself to these offices, he would dress in a tie and brown suit, he would not make jokes, he would not be a jazz musician for those few hours, and he too would ask about Papa, he would lie and say that Mama was ill, or dying, that she needed to see Papa one last time, he would stand with his hands folded innocently before him and watch the heads shake slowly, "We know nothing yet," they would say. "Give us time."

And so he would go home, back to their apartment with the faded rugs and his few treasured jazz albums, his pictures of

Louis Armstrong and Thelonious Monk on his bedroom wall, and his mama would look expectantly up at him and he would say only that the people in the offices thought they might have a lead, soon they would locate Papa, it was a white lie his mama never failed to pretend to believe.

Sometimes Mama would take down the huge atlas, a wedding present from old, untraveled Aunt Anna. She would survey the world, slowly turning the big pages, letting her finger hover uncertainly over distant cities, it was like a great game, it brought a smile to her face. And then she would say, "Paris," looking sadly into his eyes and trying to picture her son living in a city wholly of her imagining, a city that was more a state of mind, an impossible world whose reality she could never have envisaged. "You and your friend Andrzej must one day go to Paris."

So Mama had insisted on it; he was to leave Poland as soon as she had saved enough money to pay this man and that, anything was possible if you had the cash; they would help him get out, he would go to Paris and make something of his life, he and Heidi and their good friends Andrzej and Ludmilla. By the time they left there were greased palms all over Warsaw, the men in leather coats were in a celebratory mood, perhaps they knew that Wozzeck would end up working for the miserly Gino, that in his own curious way he would never escape.

"I think the shops here are wonderful," said Heidi, breaking the silence.

"I'll say this for the West," said Blotnik, gazing down at his feet, curiously shod in black vinyl things he had bought some years earlier at the Marché aux Puces, "the footwear is better, as is the state of dentistry. This, however, does not apply to England, where everyone is a toothless cripple."

"I was thinking only in general terms of the quality of life here," remarked Kupki.

"Oh well," said Wozzeck.

"A different matter entirely," said Bindler, pointing at the ceiling. "Upward mobility." Then, straining his neck to look at something on the wall behind him, he asked, "And who is the Negro?"

"Thelonious Monk," said Wozzeck. "A very great musician and collector of hats."

Bindler gazed at the other posters on the walls, as if he had never before noticed them. "There are Negroes everywhere."

"Black men make the best jazz musicians," Jerzy noted, putting on his mirrored glasses. "Black men and Russians. Isn't that so, Frau Goering, my little Luftwaffe lily?"

Heidi's mother momentarily lifted her eyes to him and returned to her sewing. She knew in her heart he was in for a bad end, she did.

Later, while Bindler was about to begin a third game of chess with Fetler, while Ludmilla and Heidi were trying on the hostess's clothes in the bedroom, Kupki and Wozzeck stood in the kitchen and discussed the future.

"You haven't told her yet?"

"I need time," said Wozzeck.

"Time, time, time, that's all I hear from you."

"It takes time."

"You've been saying that for twenty-five years."

"I still need time."

"This place really is a dump," said Kupki, glancing at the mold that had formed baroque patches on the ceiling. "A shit-house from the word go."

"You are certain everything is guaranteed?"

"We can't lose, it is an absolutely sure thing, a matter of supply and demand."

"Really," Wozzeck said doubtfully.

"Have I ever in my life lied to you?"

Jerzy thought for a moment. "Six times," he said.

"I'll go in and tell her, then."

Wozzeck took hold of his arm and pressed him against the door of the refrigerator, on which was taped a food-spattered photograph of Bessie Smith bleeding ketchup from her forehead. "I'll tell her when I think she's ready to hear it. Right now Heidi's going through a difficult period, she is like a stick of dynamite, she is living in a twilight world between reality and the movies. This week she has been the French lieutenant's woman, a real pain in the backside."

He released Kupki. They sat across from each other at the kitchen table. Schumann's "Papillons" began playing on the stereo in the living room.

"That is Heidi's record," said Wozzeck. "She says it reminds her of home."

"Does she still cry about it?"

"She and her mother, together. You think it is easy living with the old lady? Heidi is different, she is my wife, she is like my right arm. But the matriarch is a different matter. When I sit down to practice she stares at me and shakes her head, she calls me decadent, she prays for my downfall."

"Ludmilla weeps too," said Kupki. "I say to her, 'What is the matter with you, my little cauliflower, how can you cry over your home since you were so bloody happy to leave it?'"

"Heidi weeps for her papa. Heidi's mama weeps for him too. He was a concert pianist, he used to play poker with Furtwängler. Then they got him in one of their purges."

"What, the East Germans purge innocent musicians?"

"He wasn't so innocent, he became a British agent during a concert tour."

Fetler strolled in, his hands thrust deep into his pockets. "Fritzi Bindler is untrustworthy," he said, glancing warily at the picture of Charlie Mingus taped over the oven.

"He is a miser, that is all," said Wozzeck. "The fact that he is a Berliner only colors your perception of him."

"I let it go when he moved a pawn when I wasn't looking. But to replace the queen I had taken five minutes earlier is asking for big trouble. What are you talking about now, jazz music for a change, or are you plotting a murder?"

Kupki rose from his chair and left the room. Jerzy gazed at the wall and began nodding his head in time to a silent rhythm. "Da-dee," he began to sing, "da-dum." He looked up at Fetler: "It's a tune I wrote last year. One day when I am a living legend I shall record it. It's called 'To Those Who Sit and Wait.'"

* * *

Once again Kupki knocked on Wozzeck's door. "Jerzy!" he cried. "It is I, Andrzej!"

A voice from a neighboring apartment shouted *"Foutez-moi la paix!"* before what sounded like a television set was thrown at the wall.

But Wozzeck was at that moment standing on a beach, gazing out to sea. The air was warm. Palm trees shuddered and sighed in the breeze. Aeroflot jets winged their way to Kabul over the waves. In the distance he could hear a machine—*boom boom boom*—approaching him. He began to sink into the sand. The machine—*boom boom*—was coming closer. Other bathers abandoned their hampers and towels and fled the scene of the crime. A Chinaman shouted at Wozzeck in Polish and then threw himself into the sea. *Boom boom* went the machine, there was a sudden explosion, Jerzy opened his eyes slightly and saw Kupki.

"You should have told me you would leave the door unlocked," said Andrzej. "Your neighbors wish to murder me. I think I must have disturbed their sleep. What, you find this funny?"

Wozzeck laughed to himself. "I was just thinking," he said. He turned on his side, put on his dark glasses, slid a cigarette out of the pack on his bedside packing crate. "Last night I had a crazy dream, you wish to hear of it, yes?"

"No thank you."

"I dreamed about some Chinaman. I don't remember what he was doing in my dream, but nevertheless, *voilà*, a Chinaman it was. My mama used to say that if you dreamed of a Chinaman you had to beware of ladders, boiled chicken, and blind men."

"And where is Heidi?" asked Kupki.

"She had to go to work early today." Wozzeck drew on his Gitane and coughed into his fist. "This is the day everyone has to clean the cinema. It is a most amusing job, cleaning the cinema, you should see the crap she has discovered there, packs of cigarettes, popcorn, spent .44 cartridges, human shit, condoms—once she even found a guy's finger during that big Judy Garland festival they ran last year. They are preparing a new program there, that revival of *The French Lieutenant's Woman* is no longer on, thank God." He rose, and trying to pull on his trousers, displayed his small pale buttocks to Kupki. "This week they are running their annual Jerry Lewis festival. I'll have to dig out the straightjacket tonight."

"I picked up the goods this morning," said Kupki, indicating two largish and well-sealed cartons that sat beside him. "I had to carry these up four flights of stairs, your elevator wasn't working, as usual."

Wozzeck went into the kitchen. "It only operates if you hit the little box under the buttons with your fist. If you hit it in the wrong place it plunges to earth at a rate of five hundred miles per second. That means before you can even cry out for your mama you have become a human crêpe. Many of the tenants have made use of such an efficient suicide machine, the Polish secret police should only know about it. You want an egg? I am having an egg."

"Have you told her yet?" asked Kupki.

Wozzeck cracked his egg over a frying pan. He gazed seraphically at yet another photo of Thelonious Monk and a moment later at the gel surrounding his yolk, as if searching for a shared resemblance between the two enigmatic images. "The egg is not cooking," he said, spilling it into a bag of rubbish.

"I got the goods," said Kupki.

"Oh yes?"

"We can start deliveries today. You mean you still haven't told Heidi?"

Wozzeck broke another egg into the pan and drummed his fingers on the counter. "Give me time," he said.

"I'm expecting a quick turnover."

"My egg is not cooking again. It is funny, yes? Maybe we need some hot music." He went into the living room and returned a moment later. Art Blakey and the Jazz Messengers began playing "A Night in Tunisia," *rattatattatatatta* went the drums.

"Your mother-in-law, she is not here either?"

"She is sometimes afraid of staying in the apartment alone with me when Heidi is at work. She thinks I am a dangerous man, a dope fiend, a devotee of motorcycles and pornography, little does she know what really goes on inside my twisted mind. So she spends the day shopping at Inno and attending party meetings. Oh man, am I ever on to her."

"Perhaps you are being a little hard on the old woman."

"My egg, it is still not frying."

"I think you have forgotten to turn on the cooker," suggested the philosopher.

"Oh, the old lady is all right, really, ah, my egg is sizzling. But it is hard to forgive the Germans for invading Poland. I'm not too crazy about the Russians either, now that I think of it."

"So why did you marry Heidi?"

Wozzeck stared at Kupki, he did not like all these questions. "Because I was in love with her, you stupid bastard. Be cool, my egg is done. Ah, it is well done, I think." He slid the shriveled remains onto a plate and sat across from Kupki at the table. "Of course I don't hold it against Heidi, that would be unfair, no? I mean, she didn't destroy Warsaw."

"Neither did her father, who was playing poker with Furtwängler."

Wozzeck shook his fork at his friend. "One never knows about these shady maestros. So what is in the boxes—stereos, computers, grenade-launchers, jet engines?"

Kupki shrugged, he hadn't a clue. "All I was told is that we have to deliver them at two o'clock to an address in Montparnasse."

"Yes, and then?"

"We get paid for our trouble. Is good, no?"

Wozzeck rose to make coffee just as the kettle whistled out a perfect B-flat. For a brief moment he saw in his mind's eye his mama back in Warsaw, leafing through an album of photographs and quietly weeping over a snapshot of his father standing in front of the printing works, his arms crossed, a wide smile on his face, Mama's favorite picture of him. Where is Papa now? he often wondered, was he in prison? A rehabilitation camp on the edge of a windswept plain? Jerzy had of course heard about these centers of uncertainty, limbos for the lost souls of the State. Even though they were said not to exist they were often the talk of the Constanta. One of Kupki's professors at the university was said to have been sent to one, one day he was lecturing, chatting away and breaking chalk against the blackboard, and the next morning another man was standing in his place, you were not supposed to notice, even though the tone of the discussions had undergone subtle changes and the man was six inches shorter and bearded.

Or had Papa perhaps shaken off the State, as one rids oneself of an addiction, and traded it for the clandestine freedom of some underground movement, unable to show his face in the familiar streets of Warsaw or the church in which he had been married? And did he know what his son was up to, that he was being paid a pittance for playing "Strangers in the Night" for a Corsican gangster and his cronies, was he aware that his son was even alive, in Paris, free and yet not free because he could barely afford to pay his rent?

The government back home ... Wozzeck always thought of it as a huge machine full of gears and wheels and belts, a grand complexity made up of parts from old tanks, a product of the scrap heaps of past wars, a mechanism so intricately designed that before you could make any sense of it at all you would have been swallowed whole by the thing, only to reappear six months later wearing a uniform and a smile and surrounded by an entirely new set of friends....

And there was something else, that man Papa was supposed to meet, all these questions were like an itch under the skin, this man who wanted to speak to him, a friend perhaps, a new acquaintance, someone he thought he could trust?

Wozzeck sat down again, he was not quite himself, and listened for a moment to the thundering drum solo, *boomboomboomboomratatshish*, a great storm that seemed to be exploding in twenty different places at once. "This man ..." he said quietly. "This man, this man who told you to deliver these things, you know him, yes, or is he a total stranger, come, tell me."

"I met him in a café."

"Ah."

"What is this 'Ah?'"

"You have seen his credentials, he is on the level?"

"Probably not."

"Ah, good, now I feel much better, the very idea of working for some legitimate businessman has always made me uneasy."

"Look," said Kupki as he took out his pipe. "We work for him only a month, maybe two. By that time we'll have enough money to keep us going for at least a year."

"And what is he paying for this one job, your mysterious employer?"

"One thousand francs."

Wozzeck set down his cup and looked at his friend. "A thousand francs just for delivering a couple of boxes?"

"Amazing, no?"

Wozzeck went into the bedroom and stared at the cartons and did not notice any diamonds spilling out of them, it did not make sense, "We're not supposed to open them," Kupki was saying.

"One thousand, just for delivering these two boxes?"

"One thousand."

"And then what, Philosopher, I come back and find all my records stolen?"

"Oh, there'll be more deliveries, he has even guaranteed me that our wages will soon go up, the sky is the limit, he said."

Wozzeck opened a drawer and withdrew a carving knife, "I want to see what the bodies look like."

"Don't be ridiculous, there aren't any bodies."

"So what is it?"

"Goods," said Kupki.

"Goods?"

"Goods."

By half-past four they were a thousand francs richer. It had all gone so easily. The taxi had dropped them in front of the address on the rue de Vaugirard, they had rung the bell, a man had them leave the cartons inside his door, some banknotes were passed, and before they knew it they were sitting in a bistro, eating sandwiches and drinking Belgian beer, while a man in a gray suit and dark glasses read his newspaper and kept a watchful eye on them, suddenly life was like a film.

* * *

A week later Kupki and Wozzeck were on their way to a garage in Belleville, a medieval institution located off the rue Saint Fargeau that rang with the sound of metal striking metal punctuated by dull thuds, all the doors were shut, it was a mystery to Wozzeck. They were to deliver a small parcel of rare books to a man named Le Grand, Wozzeck suspected it was in reality not a small parcel of rare books, it was clear to him in a flash that Le Grand could not even write his name, much less read for enjoyment and instruction a first edition of *A l'ombre des jeunes filles en fleurs* or whatever, "*M'ci*," said Le Grand, passing them fifteen hundred in small notes and wandering off with his eighteen-inch wrench.

"I don't understand this," said Wozzeck after they had returned to a more salubrious quarter and sat in a café, "some guy gives you this parcel, we deliver it and rake in the cash. What, you think this is all legal?"

"Don't ask questions."

"What questions? I am only making an observation. First it was hairnets"—the man in the rue de Vaugirard had exclaimed, "Ah, the hairnets!" taking instant possession of the parcels—"now it's rare books, I am beginning to think it was not hairnets or rare books, that is what I think."

He could see that even Kupki was having his doubts, it always takes philosophers a bit longer to work things out for themselves, first they have to establish to their satisfaction that the world actually exists, then follows a debate about the possibility of a deity, then an exploration of personal identity, and only then is there time to wonder about hairnets and rare books, he could see Kupki was still stuck on the question of the origin of the universe, he was scratching his chin, "Look," he said.

"*Deux bières*," Wozzeck announced to the *garçon*.

"Look, I don't care what we're delivering. All I know is that last week I was sitting in the Flore and this man sits down at my table. He's well-dressed. He's polite."

"He's Vito Corleone," observed Wozzeck.

"He asks me if I and a friend wish to make a little money on the side."

"Do I have to hear your lecture again on the differences between Poland and the West?"

"This is how things are done here, you don't ask questions, you make as much money as you can and then you enjoy it."

"And this jibes with what your philosophers say, what, it was Hegel, perhaps on one of his drunken binges?"

"It has nothing to do with philosophy. I am thinking only of myself and Ludmilla. It is what I call the concept of personal greed."

Six days later the man once again made contact with Kupki and requested that he and his friend deliver two small parcels to a suite at the Crillon, in return for which they would receive the sum of two thousand francs. It took Kupki three hours to track down his friend. First he was not at home, then he was not at the café on the corner, and it was only when he reached the record shop all the way down in the *sixième*, a shop he knew was patronized by Wozzeck, that he found him, standing in front of a bin full of record albums, listening to his Walkman and bopping in place, "Oh man," he said to Kupki, "would I like this one." He indicated an American reissue of *The Amazing Bud Powell*, Volume II, priced at a hundred and twenty francs, it was outrageous, Bud Powell had died insane and now his music was fetching a small fortune, Bud Powell must be spinning in his pauper's grave, thought Wozzeck, just like Mozart in his.

"We've got another delivery to make," said Kupki, and suddenly Wozzeck saw no reason to complain, all questions had disappeared, this was the life, oh man was it ever.

There was some difficulty in gaining admission to the Crillon, as it was obvious that the concierge and two other employees at once suspected them of being terrorists, jewel thieves, junkies, tramps, and besides Elizabeth Taylor was spending the week there, they could be journalists inquiring about facelifts and the like.

"We have to make a delivery," said Kupki. Already he had taken Wozzeck aside and begged him to allow him, Kupki, to do the talking, Wozzeck was entirely too unpredictable.

The concierge conferred with the head of hotel security, a man who looked as if he ran a high-class male brothel, Wozzeck could hardly contain himself for fear of the brute. "We shall see that the gentleman in Suite Eighteen receives the parcels," said the security man, and it was apparent that the moment Wozzeck and Kupki were out of their sight he would call in the bomb squad, he did not like their looks.

"Look, dig, we have to do it ourselves," said Wozzeck.

"Shut up," hissed Kupki. He turned to the security man. "Please understand that we have been asked to deliver these personally."

"And I must get that Bud Powell record before the shop closes," added Wozzeck. "It is a matter of life and death."

They did not know the identity of the recipient of the parcels, only his suite number, and a compromise was reached which allowed Kupki and Wozzeck to remain in the lobby while the concierge made the delivery himself. Ten minutes later he was handing Kupki a thick envelope and hinting that they should get the hell out of this palace of luxury before people began complaining, though of course he did not put it quite that way, a smile and a hand indicating the door was worth a thousand words, a nice tip on top of two grand in francs.

* * *

"Two thousand francs!" Wozzeck was saying as he stumbled around the living room and listened to Bud Powell and tried to avoid Kupki's legs, which were sprawled out in front of him, the philosopher having passed out ten minutes earlier.

Heidi had taken it all very well, the news of Wozzeck's new job, considering she had at one time harbored much higher hopes for her husband, picturing him performing as her father had in the great concert halls of Europe, or else conducting the Berlin Philharmonic in place of a disgraced Herbert von Karajan. "It is so funny, I think," she told Ludmilla when they went into the kitchen to make coffee. "Really, Jerzy and Andrzej have stooped to such a ridiculous low. With Andrzej you might expect such a thing, a degree in philosophy prepares you for doing nothing much else than selling the public cheap goods and telling everyone they are pure gold. But Jerzy is a musician, he is like Schwarzkopf, completely devoted to his art, he should be giving master classes instead of delivering hairnets."

"Hairnets!" Wozzeck cried for the tenth time that evening. "We deliver hairnets and books and they give us the pot of gold at the end of the rainbow, something is rotten in Denmark, I should be thinking."

"Your husband is making an idiot of himself," said Heidi's mama as she came into the kitchen. She was wearing, as she invariably did when entertaining at home, her old flowered dressing gown. Made by slave labor, Wozzeck had always thought, and carrying the label of Kultur-Mode, Karl-Marx-Stadt.

"Well, I think Andrzej has made a brilliant decision," said Ludmilla. "For years I have watched the poor man being pushed around by these French people, there is no reason why he cannot make his fortune the way everyone else does in the West."

Heidi shrugged and took down four cups from the shelf. She had always envied Ludmilla, not only for her dark good looks—indeed she believed her friend was part gypsy and thus invested with some special sexual power—she had often caught Jerzy gazing at her legs—but also for her job, which she had held for nearly two years, at a Polish cultural institute on the Right Bank. On the surface it seemed merely an arm of the government, but in truth was allied to the Solidarity movement and funded by various eminent French figures who spent most of their time sitting in cafés and writing essays for obscure journals and the capitalist press. The institute was run by an attractive woman named Irina Lapicki, who was also a feminist and enjoyed speaking indiscreetly about her bodily functions when not plotting to castrate such luminaries of the masculine sex as Jean-Paul Belmondo and Gérard Depardieu. There one could pick up leaflets discussing Polish literature, theater, and cinema, and whenever a new Polish film was opening in Paris, it was the institute's responsibility to help publicize it. Andrzej Wajda was a frequent visitor, and his photograph was featured prominently on the wall above Ludmilla's desk. Occasionally sinister-looking middle-aged Poles in cheap suits would pay a visit to the institute, cast an eye on the pamphlets laid out neatly on the table at the door, and question Ludmilla about the other employees. But Ludmilla had been forewarned by Irina that such spies might stop by, and so she would respond, breezily and with a salacious smile, with an assortment of prearranged lies. And sometimes, late in the afternoon, young Poles would gather in Irina's back office, whisper among themselves, and leave an hour later carrying bundles of leaflets and posters hidden beneath their coats as if, instead of walking out onto the rue de Rivoli, they were still somewhere in Warsaw, sneaking around under the eyes of the police.

Ludmilla vicariously enjoyed participating in this secret movement and was often seen sporting a small Solidarity badge. Her nationality had also, at the time of the imposition of martial law, earned her the admiration and sexual attentions of certain Parisian undergraduates, as if by sleeping with her they were somehow taking a central role in a great historical moment.

Heidi, however, was not politically motivated, and instead took refuge in her work. There was something comforting in the notion of spending day after day living in a world of make-believe, of flying saucers and aliens and the French lieutenant's woman ("Ach, does she have problems," she told Jerzy after her first viewing of the film) and huge sharks that tore off people's limbs when not eating old Buicks; sitting in the darkness of the rear of the cinema, sucking on jujubes, she knew she was safe from harm. Sometimes she was like Jerzy, finding herself confusing life with what pretended to be art, or rather would suddenly discover herself detached from her surroundings, taking part in, but in truth only observing, the conversations she was sharing with Wozzeck or Ludmilla or even her own mama, and this too would give her a tiny frisson, an eerie chill that made her spine shiver, as it had in reverse when for the thirty-fifth time she had watched *The Godfather* and had momentarily forgotten that Santino had not really been riddled with machine-gun bullets but a moment later, and in the guise of James Caan, had stood up, laughed it off, made a joke, and walked off the set for a glass of tea and perhaps a bowl of *chlodnik*.

She and Ludmilla returned to the living room with the coffee and cake. Kupki was laid out on the sofa, snoring, his hands in his trouser pockets. "And where is Jerzy?" Heidi asked. And perhaps she was sometimes quite right to view life as a movie, for at that moment Wozzeck was making his way to the club, the earphones of his Walkman stuck to his head, while a man not yet known to him was following this little Pole, a leisurely thirty paces behind.

* * *

On the way he decided he would lead off with "Strangers in the Night," which was such a big hit with the owner of the club because, he thought, it was closely associated with an American singer renowned the world over as a friend of hoodlums and confidant of presidents. Then he'd follow that with "April in Paris," "Summertime," "Night and Day," "Some Enchanted Evening"—all the usual tunes that fell within the guidelines laid down by the dangerous Gino and his late predecessor. Although tonight he felt like taking a risk, playing a forty-three-minute version of Coltrane's "Afro-Blue," laying on the dissonance and block chords and perhaps even topping it all off with a screaming fit and a lecture on Black Power and an appeal to revolutionaries, wherever they may be, he decided at the last minute not to do so, as he might very well end up, albeit over two thousand francs in the black, a bloated carcass somewhere in the Paris sewers.

Yes, yes, he could see the audience tonight was going to be responsive, it was clear from the start, you could see it at once. There was that pair of adolescents, the boy's hand mysteriously stuck between the girl's thighs as he whispered sugary nothings into her sweet little ear, a pair that wouldn't give a damn about the music, not even if Jerzy took off his clothes to play it and offered free joints and an assortment of barbiturates to them. Then there was the usual assortment of bewildered Americans in berets, desperate for hamburgers at any cost, who would return home thinking that here in this stinking little hole on the Boul' Mich' they had tasted something of the real

Paris, and who yet each and every time gave Wozzeck a tremendous hand, so that afterward he would feel guilty and play for no one else but them. And finally there were the regulars, mustachioed Corsicans who smoked cigars and ate nuts and drank sweet aperitifs and through slitted eyes watched Wozzeck as if at any moment they might blow him off the face of the earth. Sometimes these men would disappear into the kitchen next to Gino's office. Sometimes they would return, and sometimes they would never be seen again, except perhaps between the two halves of a baguette. Each Friday Wozzeck had to collect his wages in this office, a small paneled room furnished with a desk and a chair and a small bed. On the walls were photographs of smiling naked women—women, it was rumored among the kitchen staff, that Gino had taken into slavery and who, after hours, in that uncertain corridor between night and day, were released from their chains and made to perform sexual acts with Gino himself, his brother Rico, and (according to chef Belleto, the hamburger king himself) a bull known as Hemingway. There was talk of a crime empire bigger than the Sûreté and pornography released from the club's office that reached printing runs greater than the works of André Gide; drugs were mentioned, gun-running, even that the club was a front for a vast pool of mercenaries, ready at a moment's notice, and that should some insane ruler somewhere in the world need an army of fifteen or twenty thousand armed and bloodthirsty criminals, all he need do was ring up Le Hamburger-Hot and politely ask for Gino.

Or so they said.

Little of this fazed Wozzeck, especially now that he was about to earn a fortune just by delivering hairnets. As he mechanically went through the chord progressions of "April in Paris" he thought about what he might do in the future. There was his age-old dream of moving to Newark, New Jersey, of course, just to be where he thought all jazz musicians lived, in a tenement alive with cockroaches and smeared with graffiti, from which he would venture to Manhattan each evening to play long, sweaty sets at the Blue Note or the Village Vanguard. But he had often spoken to Heidi about this scheme and had decided that, as she categorically refused to join him in the slums of America, he would set aside his plan until she could be persuaded of its innate brilliance. In the meantime he would send his mama some money so that this winter she would not have to wear her twenty-year-old boots that she could now donate to the museum.

And so he played: "Summertime," "Hernando's Hideaway (Olé)," and so on, until the moment came for his break. He took his usual seat and was brought his usual beer and, as always, he switched on his Walkman and tonight listened to Bird's "Ornithology," which sounded especially hot to his burning ears.

The second set was nothing less than a success. Certain people who he knew were ardent fans of his music, *clochards* and perverts the lot of them, stopped by and cheered each piece and then went off to expose themselves up by the Beaubourg or else to do a little slashing deep in the Bois de Boulogne. Afterward, impatient to return home to Heidi, he ran to the Saint Michel métro station and—stroke of luck—caught a train just as it was about to leave. It was when he changed lines at Réaumur Sébastopol and was on his way to his stop at Gambetta that he realized he was being followed. And what made matters worse was that his pursuer was the very man who, for at least ten minutes that evening, had been peering at him through the window at the club. Wozzeck discreetly switched off his Walkman—Mingus's sassy *Tijuana Moods* album—and with a look of sweet innocence surveyed the car, only to realize he was alone with this man. Not an unusual thing, of course, not at that hour, most people would have welcomed such peace, especially since, after midnight, the métro traditionally fell into the hands of the unbalanced hordes of Paris.

The man was sitting at the far end of the train. He wore a blue suit and a neatly trimmed mustache and at intervals threw brief glances at Wozzeck. It occurred to Jerzy that it might be worth a try if he stood up, assumed a belligerent pose, and asked the man straight out if he was watching him. On the other hand he thought it prudent not to do so, he was too young to die, and the idea of Heidi being summoned to the morgue in the middle of the night to identify a butchered corpse did not especially appeal to him. Therefore he remained seated until the train stopped at Arts et Métiers. And then, at the last moment, Wozzeck sprang from his seat and found himself on the deserted platform. He sat down beneath a huge film poster of Belmondo in his underpants and waited for the next train, which, because it was nearly midnight, arrived only thirteen minutes later. He took a seat in a car and sat down—safety in numbers—beside an attractive woman, who, of course, being the only other passenger and suspecting him of being a rapist, at once got up and moved to another seat. The train stopped at Temple, then République, and at Parmentier the woman got out and left him alone in the car. And when he looked up he saw the man in the blue suit sitting at the opposite end, staring at him. Wozzeck once again switched off his music and wondered what he could use to defend himself: his keys, his shoes, the little cassette player, his head—he possessed nothing at all, while this man, he suspected, was armed to the teeth with brass knuckles, submachine guns, machetes, electroshock equipment purchased from the Polish secret police, mustard-gas canisters, grenades, and boxing gloves. Wozzeck perspired and watched his life pass before his eyes: his childhood days in Warsaw, endless Saturday afternoons strolling with Kupki, his first, second, and third loves, the first time he had heard Thelonious Monk. How vivid and pathetic it all seemed as the train raced toward Père Lachaise and his own inevitably gruesome end. When it came to that stop he casually rose from his seat, stepped out and, as the man exited from the other door of the carriage, returned to the train and smiled to himself as the stranger was left far behind him, standing by the plastic seats on the platform.

And Wozzeck didn't see him again, at least not until he got off at Gambetta to find the man sitting and waiting for him.

# 2

NOW THAT HE IS IN LONDON, IN THIS APARTMENT IN Hampstead, now that things have gone from bad to worse, Wozzeck looks back on his years in Paris as perhaps the happiest of his life. Oh certainly, *bien sûr,* it hadn't been easy, not for a single moment, the money hadn't exactly been pouring in, and yet somehow he and Heidi had enjoyed their meager existence, for the stink of corruption had not yet invaded their lives.

How complicated things are now....

His memory, for instance. He can easily remember his boyhood in Warsaw, or at least the first eight years of it, for afterward things had begun to go downhill, there was that man, that man who wanted to speak to Papa: he is wondering if it was then the seed of tragedy had been planted in his soul.

How willingly Papa went.... Had he just given up?

Funny thing, he thinks. Funny how distant Paris seems to him now that so much has happened and he is in an apartment in Hampstead, in London. There was that man, the man on the métro, and Wozzeck is having difficulty getting the chronology in reasonable order.

He attempts to trace his itinerary of that night, now he is lost in the network of stations, now he is getting out at Gambetta, he sees the man sitting in a seat, a man in a blue suit and mustache, and the man is not moving, even though Wozzeck is making a mad dash for the exit.

Curious now, Wozzeck has summoned up the courage to approach the man, there is no sign of acknowledgement, and Wozzeck thinks, this is Death, this is how it ends, late at night in a deserted métro station, a death unwitnessed, a quiet and pathetic end. And he thinks of Heidi and his mama, Kupki and Ludmilla and even Heidi's mama, whom he had so abused, even though he is certain she had been a washroom attendant at the Reichstag.

He looks carefully at Death, examines him from every angle, notices the ring on his right hand (so Death is a Freemason, is he), the lengthening shadow on the chin, the wristwatch that must have set him back at least five thousand francs. He tries to read Death's mind and wonders what images play upon the interior of Death's skull, a triptych of Hieronymous Bosch, scenes from Hitchcock's *Psycho*, an antique tomb in some arcadian paradise....

"*Bonsoir*," he says to Death, and "*Ça va?*" but Death has nothing to say to him, Death is mute, and for a moment Jerzy thinks that Death, like those beggars on the métro, might hand him a card speaking of deafness and hunger and hard luck, while all the while your wallet is disappearing up his sleeve.

It is only when he touches Death's shoulder that he realizes Death has died. And when he catches sight of that long slim knife emerging from Death's back, and even wraps his fingers around the handle, he knows he has crossed over to the other side, he has descended into the underworld, he is lost forever.

He lifts his head, for he is in London, and looks across the room at Kupki, who may not be there, he can no longer tell what is real, and so he demands verification. "Did I really see that man, Kupki?" he asks, and "Do you remember Hort, our principal at school, and the plaster bust of Lenin on his desk?"

But Kupki is not there to answer, he is being held hostage, and so there is only emptiness, vacancy, memory. And blood. Lots of blood. And thus Wozzeck will never know for certain the answers he has been seeking. What is jazz? he wonders. What is death? But there is only the echo of his own confused thoughts, the sound of a city that will never take notice of his life, or death. So this is London, and the Northern Line rumbles hundreds of feet beneath this apartment in Hampstead, tourists are standing up at the gates of the British Museum, a silver Rolls-Royce inches silently along a crowded A4, a Chinese family in Soho is in mourning. Wozzeck has become yet one more insignificant speck in the vast universe.

* * *

But the next morning—for he is once again remembering that past in which he'd always had a choice to do this, to say that, indeed to scream "No" when all that was demanded was a simple "Yes"—he told Kupki about his nightmare journey through the lower Parisian depths. He told him also that he had not been able to fall asleep until dawn, that it was not only Heidi's talking in her sleep that had kept him awake, quoting lines from old Jerry Lewis comedies and, worse, laughing at them, but rather the thought that he had been followed and that the man who had been following him had been murdered, very nearly before his eyes. "And to make matters worse," he added, "when I did fall asleep I dreamed that Fritzi Bindler was sitting on my head. What, you find this funny?"

"Come on, we must make our delivery, they are expecting us, we have to report to the head office."

"You must be insane."

Kupki tore off the end of his croissant and plunged it into his steaming *café au lait.* "I don't find two thousand francs beyond the scope of human logic."

They arrived at the office at noon exactly. It was located in an anonymous block of apartments in Boulogne-Billancourt, south of the Bois de Boulogne, at the end of a long and tedious ride on the métro. During the trip Wozzeck listened to a tape by the Art Ensemble of Chicago, and this helped keep him awake, especially as the batteries in his Walkman were running down and the music no longer sounded like music but rather like Napoleon's armies plundering Moscow, he could hear the screams of Gorbachev's ancestors. Kupki perused the names in the foyer and pressed the button beneath one that read simply "UniRex." A buzzer sounded and Andrzej pushed open the heavy glass door.

As they rode up in the lift Kupki said, "I think you will be impressed."

"Oh, go to hell," said Wozzeck, switching off his music and turning away.

A young woman in a thin dress opened the door and smiled as she shook their hands. "And you must be the pianist," she said to Wozzeck. "Andrzej has told us so much about you."

"He has? Why is this?"

"He says you are a talented man, full of inspiration and soul."

Wozzeck could not recall when he had last seen such a beautiful woman, he fell in love with her blue eyes and blond hair and long legs, and that smile, my God, that smile. And he thought that, if ever left alone with her, he too would confess everything, tell her intimate details about his friends, even throw himself at her feet and request to be made her slave. He could see why writers the world over created beautiful women, they so distracted the audience from idiotic plots and typographical errors. He watched as she disappeared behind another door. He and Kupki sat on the sofa and looked briefly at each other.

"What, you tell strange women the secrets of my life?" said Wozzeck.

"I've never seen her before. Oh, I may have mentioned to that guy I told you about that you played piano and so on."

"Just shut up, will you."

Kupki raised a finger: "Two thousand. That means another thousand for each of us."

"Now you are talking."

They were joined by a man in a gray suit and dark glasses. Wozzeck estimated the man's age to be anywhere between forty and two hundred sixty-three, it was impossible to tell, what with his shades and probable facelift. Wozzeck also wondered whether the man had had little tucks taken in his buttocks, it was all the rage among the idle rich, though he would not dare inquire, it was asking for big trouble and a possible kick in the backside.

The man offered his hand to each of them and sat in an armchair constructed from sheets of leather and stainless steel tubing, designed in Milan by wealthy sadists. "My name is not important," he said. "The fact that you have volunteered to work for me means that we are all friends here, and thus formalities can be dispensed with. Please sit down, make yourselves comfortable. My assistant will bring drinks and a small luncheon in a few minutes. I believe you are a musician, Monsieur Wozzeck. Jazz, I am told."

"Yes, that is so," said Wozzeck uncomfortably.

"You are a pianist. You are regularly employed?"

"He plays at a club on the Boul' Mich'," volunteered Kupki. He could not seem to mind his own business lately, it occured to Wozzeck.

"Ah, the Boulevard Saint Michel, yes, of course. You are a most fortunate man to have such an interesting profession." The man rose, went to a desk, took a cigar from a box. Then he picked up another, smaller box and held it out to his guests. Forgetting himself for a moment, Wozzeck scooped up a handful of cigarettes and stuffed them into the pocket of his leather jacket while Kupki began to make excuses—"My friend comes from a poor family," and so forth.

"It doesn't matter," the man said, laughing drily. "He can have as many as he likes. Monsieur Kupki, you look confused. Let me guess why. Is it because the man who has been your regular contact these past few weeks is not the same man who now sits before you? Perhaps you think that we resemble each other a little. Perhaps this is so. No, no, I do not normally deal directly with our employees. The man you met was only my administrative director. Ah, here are the drinks."

The vision of beauty placed a tray on the table and poured out three vodka martinis. "Your health, gentlemen," said their host.

By the time they finished their third drink Wozzeck was quite convinced the events of the previous night had not taken place. He had even broached the subject to their host, describing in vivid detail his trip on the métro and the state of the corpse, and there was laughter all around and much merriment, and Kupki even took the opportunity to give a brief lecture on the philosophical implications of death, how Russell would have reacted if he had been in Wozzeck's shoes (with calm acceptance and a cup of tea), and what Nietzsche might have done (serenely berated the corpse for not having survived), and so on, and then suddenly it seemed to Wozzeck as if the lights had gone out, and they were eating their lunch in a darkened room, though of course this was only the effect of having drunk five too many martinis. He knew he was making a fool of himself, but he hadn't eaten so well at least since Grandmama's funeral back in Warsaw, and at that moment he was quite willing to deliver whatever the man asked him to, bodies, cows, the blonde, even blood plasma and coffins full of Transylvanian dirt.

"I am delighted you enjoyed your meal. I am even more pleased that you have decided to continue working for me and my company. As I mentioned, by way of my administrative director, to Monsieur Kupki, today I shall be willing to pay you each one thousand francs, with the understanding that if I am satisfied with your work I shall not only continue to make use of your services, but also raise your commission in the very near future. I ask you only not to divulge to anyone whom you are working for, nor to lead anyone back to this office. Should you disobey me the consequences could be most unpleasant. This is understood?"

Wozzeck and Kupki smiled stupidly and nodded their heads.

"I am not willing at this time to discuss the precise nature of my business, nor do I wish to answer any of the questions you might naturally have in mind. I think you are two honest young men who desire a little extra money, and because I know you are honest I shall expect you also to be loyal to me."

The woman brought two small parcels into the room and left them on the long glass table in front of the sofa. She smiled at Wozzeck and leaned against the wall by the windows, her arms crossed, raw sexuality from head to toe, thought Jerzy.

"Today," the man continued, "you will be delivering a further selection of rare books to one of our regular customers, a dear friend of mine visiting from Milano. He has, shall we say, a special interest in the esoteric writings of certain nineteenth-century authors. He is staying at the Hôtel Morel on the rue de la Huchette, Room Seventeen. If you would simply ensure that these parcels are placed in his hands you will have done your job and earned yourselves two thousand francs. When I am ready to engage you again I shall notify you in the usual fashion."

Wozzeck looked at Kupki.

"Your friend is puzzled. Undoubtedly Monsieur Kupki did not inform you as to our arrangements. Let me just say that when you are needed, one of my associates will find you and pass on the details. You see," he said, rising from his seat and moving toward his desk, "I know a great deal about both of you. I know that Monsieur Kupki tutors five individuals in preparation for their *baccalauréat*. I know where each of them lives, and I know too that his wife works at a Polish cultural institute. You, Monsieur Wozzeck, work six evenings a week at your club. I know your hours, I know too the route you take to get there and back from your apartment on the rue Stendhal. You enjoy playing there?"

"Yes and no," said Wozzeck, and he explained why yes and why no, he briefly discussed block chords and the differences between Charlie Parker and Frank Sinatra and his ilk, it was like black and white, and he could see the man did not give a damn for what he was saying, he just nodded and grinned.

"Now, you work for a man named Gino Vezzani, am I correct?"

"Yes, yes, Gino, that's right."

"Do you know him well, this Gino?"

"No, no, not at all, I simply play my piano, I do not get involved in the business of the back room."

"Another drink?"

Wozzeck held out his glass, he had spent half the day drinking vodka martinis, later he would have two beers at the club, it no longer made any difference how much more he drank, he would still come home and vomit in the sink.

"I know something of his reputation, your Monsieur Vezzani," the man in the gray suit and shades went on. "He interests me a great deal." A smile: "As do you, both of you, whose lives are open books to me. Are your papers in order?"

"Me?" said Kupki.

"I ask you again: are your papers in order?"

"Papers, yes, of course."

"And yours, Monsieur Wozzeck?"

Wozzeck sipped at his drink, took a mouthful of caviar, his head moved dully up and down, up and down.

"Yes or no, please answer my question."

"Nes," said Wozzeck, who suddenly did not like the man's tone, not one bit, he was beginning to sound like Gino.

"You mentioned something that occurred at Gambetta métro station last night, Monsieur Wozzeck. You say a man had been following you and was then murdered. Can you describe this man?"

And Wozzeck suddenly did not feel very drunk at all, he could see things with tremendous clarity, his mind struck like lightning on a scene he had hoped he would forget. He spoke of a man in a blue suit, a man about forty-five, a man with a thin mustache and expensive shiny shoes, a man who had died with his eyes wide open; a knife with a black plastic handle.

"So you murdered this man who had been following you," said the man in the gray suit and dark glasses.

"No, no, look, man, you're not catching my drift."

"I certainly must say I can't blame you. Paris has become so very dangerous, don't you think? A man like you being followed, terrorized … You did the only thing you could to save your life. This is an amazing thing, is it not?" the man said, turning to the woman. "Monsieur Wozzeck has confessed to a very serious crime. Do you not agree, Monsieur Kupki?"

"Well, I—"

"Were you there to witness the great event, Monsieur Kupki?"

"No, but I—"

"There were no witnesses, then?"

"Witnesses?" said Wozzeck.

"Witnesses," repeated the man.

"Witnesses?" Suddenly nothing was making sense, witnesses? Witnesses? He might just as well have been telling the story of Fifi the elephant and her lover Ruiz the flea for all he knew about witnesses. "No," he said, "no witnesses."

"Then I congratulate you, Monsieur Wozzeck. And I am glad to see that I was not the victim of your crime."

"But I could not hurt a fly, I am incapable even of eating a hamburger, formerly a cow, I—"

"There is no need to apologize. Let me just say that I for one shall never reveal your secret. Not as long as you remain faithful to me and my company. Do you know," he said, "I have been most rude. I have not yet formally introduced my friend here, Mademoiselle Rita."

"You can just call me Rita," said Rita, who for some reason even looked like a Rita, she could never be pegged as a Heidi or a Ludmilla, thought Wozzeck, though she might just as well have been called Vera VaVoom, her clothes seemed about to fall off her.

"Say hello to Rita, gentlemen."

"Hello, *bonjour*," said Wozzeck and Kupki.

It was then that Wozzeck realized Rita was not fully dressed, or rather she was wearing a dress, a thin one to be sure, but that underneath there was very little else but Rita herself, in the flesh so to speak, and he saw that things were taking yet another turn, whether for better or worse he could not say. And when she came over to pour the coffee he had an even better view of Rita, a great deal of Rita, nearly her entire northern hemisphere.

"Monsieur Wozzeck and Monsieur Kupki are Polish, Rita," said the sinister gray-suited man.

"How nice," she said brightly, stepping back and smiling with her teeth.

"Some years ago they escaped the communist terror to live in freedom here in the West."

"Bravo," said Rita.

"Rita is English," said the man in the gray suit and shades. "She is a former Miss West Sussex, though she hails from Kent. As you have no doubt noticed, her French is impeccable. I consider her indispensable. Do you know England, Monsieur Wozzeck?"

"Me? No, no."

"Perhaps one day you will get to know it, then. There are many sights to see in London, for instance. What would you recommend, Rita?"

"Lots of things."

"You see?" said the man. "London is full of wonders. Ah, I see it has begun to rain, and you two gentlemen have a little job to do for me. Remember, Room Seventeen, Hôtel Morel, rue de la Huchette. At that time you will be paid for your services."

* * *

That night, to celebrate their newfound wealth, Wozzeck and Kupki took their wives to an early dinner at a cafeteria on the Boulevard Montparnasse, a pigsty much patronized by impoverished émigrés with insensitive palates. There, for the price of a pack of Gitanes and a newspaper, one could eat like a hog, glutting oneself on what appeared to be freshly slaughtered *bifteck* and a mountain of *pommes frites* and great jugs of beer. Music of an indescribably banal nature played continuously from small loudspeakers set high on the walls, far beyond Wozzeck's reach.

Heidi was looking particularly beautiful, what with her short blond hair and long legs, not forgetting that smile that seemed to burn away all your worries. Other men could not keep their eyes off her; three years earlier on the Champs-Elysées Jerzy was pleased to see even one such as Alain Delon's bodyguard with his gaze glued to her backside. Ludmilla too looked ravishing, and Wozzeck could hardly control himself, she so reminded him of Lydia Kovel, his first love, who for the payment of a handful of *zlotys* had allowed him to fondle her left breast for fifteen seconds.

And, as always, when they got together like this, conversation would turn to the past, tears would be shed and everyone would begin to grow desperately nostalgic. "Sometimes," Ludmilla was saying, "sometimes I get terribly lonely here. Oh, I have wonderful friends, you and Jerzy and so on, but I really do miss Warsaw."

"I'm hip," said Wozzeck. "Martial law or not it's still home."

"Sometimes I think Paris is a jungle," said Heidi. "I feel as if someone has pulled the floor right out from under my feet, I could cry sometimes, you should see me. This afternoon at the matinée I took a customer to the wrong seat and I am sure he called me a German pig. And my mama, ach, you should see what she has to put up with sometimes. You'd think we were still at war with these animals."

Wozzeck had his own ideas about Heidi's mama, and he could not repress a smile. There had been some talk in Heidi's family about her father's activities during the war, whether he had belonged to the Party or not and so forth, but Wozzeck, as always, let his imagination go and had transformed the musician into a war criminal of the worst sort, Wozzeck privately referred to him as the Beast with Ten Fingers.

As Heidi and Ludmilla and Kupki continued to reminisce, Wozzeck could not keep himself from musing over the events of the night before. I saw the man myself, he thought, I saw Death on the Gambetta platform. And yet the man in the gray suit and shades was wrong, I didn't kill the man in the blue suit. Who killed the man in the blue suit, then, and who or what was UniRex?

"Did you ever know Katinka Grodnik?" Heidi was asking.

"Katinka Grodnik," said Ludmilla. "No, I don't think so."

"Ach, of course, you never lived in Leipzig. You remember her, Jerzy, yes?"

But Wozzeck was a million miles away, in the Café Constanta in the Old Town, playing bebop for his regular audience, secret policemen and undergraduates. How simple it had all been back then, one knew the rules, one saw the future, there were no complications, people died behind closed doors. It was just like Mama had always said, when you are young you never notice the bad things. Yet even now, sobered by hindsight, tears came to his eyes as he recalled the days of his youth, before things went bad, and he wished the future could simply be a repeat of the past. But to return to Poland now would be dangerous, even insane, people were being swallowed up by the system at a rate of ten thousand a minute, knives were being sharpened, priests murdered, jails filled, there was even a waiting list at the cemetery. "Why have you returned?" they would ask him. "So, the promise of the West has turned out to be a great illusion, has it? Good. Now that you are back in Poland we shall make an example of you." And he would disappear for five or ten years, only to reappear an automaton on Jerusalem Avenue, his soul having been appropriated by the State.

And yet he felt compelled to keep up an albeit tenuous connection with his homeland. Twice a month he wrote to his mother, often enclosing a little money to help tide her over. He would send snapshots of himself and Heidi, taken in the bright sunniness of the Buttes-Chaumont. "Smile, Heidi," he would say. "Let Mama think we are on top of the world."

Yet most of his letters remained unanswered, Wozzeck picturing them drifting from bureau to bureau and being examined for coded messages by diligent cryptographers, and thus, until it occurred to him that one day the secret police might begrudge the extra work he was costing them and take reprisals against his mother, he amused himself by thinking he was somehow slowing up the gears of the government.

And yet it was a curious thing ... Although he had quite willingly come to Paris—it was his mama's wish—he had never suspected how unprepared he would be for the experience of the West. Oh, there were certain slight similarities, all right, for instance the vast bureaucracy that seemed to have been designed by some sadistic Muscovite intent on punishing the French for having sent Napoleon to burn down his capital. And of course one made sure not to fall into the hands of the French police, they were said to rival their colleagues beyond the Berlin Wall. But how strange it was to arrive in this world in which nobody suspected you, or watched you, or even followed you, though of course there were people who followed you all over Paris, in the métro and on the boulevards, beggars and pick-pockets, one could deal with them, they were much better than the secret police. And naturally you could play what you liked on the piano, tone clusters and block chords and the like, as long as you didn't do it in Gino's club.

At first he had found himself floundering about, feeling rather lost in the big city, unsure of what to do next. Heidi, of course, knew precisely what she should do, she learned French in a month and found a job, she was the resourceful one in the family. But Wozzeck was saddened to think that Poland had somehow crippled him, leaving him only able to function in a world bounded by regulation and restriction, where it was easier living in doubt and never quite trusting anyone, where you could withdraw into the warm vastness of your imagination, or listen to Mingus, or sit in a movie and watch Randolph Scott bite the dust, it was an education in itself.

Eventually he and Kupki roused themselves and found work, and in time began to adjust to this odd new world. No one suspected them or informed on them; no stares or gray unsmiling faces behind a café window; no strangers at the door, asking for a chat. And, until now, no one following them

"Jerzy, don't you remember?" Heidi was saying. "I'm telling the Kupkis about the cabbage."

"Oh yes?"

"Don't you remember? When we first moved to Paris Jerzy tried to flush a rotten head of cabbage down the toilet."

"It's what we used to do in Warsaw."

"But I told him it's just not done here, it's not chi-chi."

"I bet Jacqueline Onassis does it."

"Don't be ridiculous, Jerzy."

"And Yves Saint-Laurent and Christian Dior and Nathalie Baye and all those other people you hold in high esteem. I can even tell you as a dead certainty that Thelonious Monk did it at least twice a week, simply for his own amusement." He looked at Kupki. "Wittgenstein did it too."

He knew that when he got like this no one wanted to know from him. At such times he would appear to be unstable, off-center, even potentially dangerous to the welfare of others. He had a ripe and vivid imagination that he utilized like a tenor sax or even his piano, stretching it to the limit, throwing off riffs, alarming his audience with his wild improvisations and making them see that here was someone who feared nothing, who was free, who if he weren't careful might suddenly burst into flames. He remembered seeing once in Krakow a Russian jazz trio who improvised with such heat, such passion and energy that even the secret police who sat here and there in the audience seemed to grow afraid, as if everything they believed in was being torn to shreds, beaten to a pulp, left to bleed to death right in front of their eyes. And he knew that when they returned to Russia they would remain free men, they would fear no one, simply because they had discovered liberation in their precious music.

"*Excusez-moi*," he said as he rose from the table and staggered to the toilet. He had drunk four huge glasses of beer and could hardly contain them, they seemed about to spill out of him, so small was he and so large the portions. The toilet, located in a small corridor near the kitchen, was designed for single occupancy and thus one was compelled to lock it from the inside, by means of a small bolt. Jerzy was in no condition to deal with complex modern inventions, and so he simply shut the door and took a seat, his privacy ensured by a small partition decorated with drawings in various hands of dripping phalluses and women's backsides. He had been there only a minute when he heard the door open and close and the bolt thrown. And then the light was switched off.

"Rocco Lunel is dead," said a voice. "He was murdered last night. Other people want to take over his territory. So tell your boss to keep away, you understand?"

"*Oui*," said Wozzeck, "*d'accord*."

"Are you armed?" the man asked him.

"*Oui*," said Wozzeck, "I have a gun."

He heard a clicking noise. "And I have a knife."

"Now I no longer have a gun," said Wozzeck as he felt the tears roll down his cheeks.

"But I still have a knife. One more bit of funny business like that and you are a dead man, you understand?"

"*Oui, oui*, perfectly, it is crystal clear."

"You play piano?" the Murderer asked. Wozzeck could hear a zipper being unzipped and the unmistakable sound of a large man urinating into what may have been the wash basin.

"Yes," said Jerzy.

"So you work for Gino. I know Gino. I can arrange things. He doesn't like people who mess with him. You know what he does to people who mess with him?"

"No."

"Try it and find out. You wouldn't want to be embroiled with Gino, would you?"

"Now that you put it that way, no."

"Good, that's fine. Remember what I told you. One more delivery in Rocco's territory and you and your skinny friend are as good as dead, okay?"

"Fine, yes, that is all right with me, a most reasonable arrangement."

Wozzeck suddenly realized that the Murderer was standing directly in front of him, in this strange artificial night. He decided to remain silent to throw him off.

"Are you there?" asked the Murderer.

Wozzeck said nothing. He could hear a foot scraping along the floor, seeking out the vulnerable parts of his poor body.

"I know you are there," the man resumed. "Your wife is a very beautiful woman. She is a sex kitten. She has a nice ass and fantastic legs, and if we don't get you first we'll mark her up for life, you understand? One more trick like that, you Polish shit ..."

Wozzeck heard the door shut. He remained in the darkness for a minute more, and was about to get up and grope his way to the door when he heard it open again. He wished he were just a Polish shit, then he could easily flush himself down the toilet to freedom.

"Wozzeck?"

Who was this?

"Wozzeck, it is I, Kupki."

"My God, you should only know what has happened—"

"Why are you in the dark, are you sick?"

"Please just switch on the light."

"Where is it?"

"How the hell am I supposed to know? There was someone in here, he threatened to kill me, to mutilate Heidi, we shall have to speak to the man."

"What man, the one who was in here? I don't understand. A man was in here with you? He has left?"

"Yes, I think so. If not, we are dead men. Our deliveries, someone is not happy with them, in fact 'not happy' is the wrong phrase, it does not convey the sheer force of this man's anger, in other words we are well and truly screwed."

"You the other Pole?" It was the Murderer.

"Oh, Christ," moaned Wozzeck.

"Who is this?" asked Kupki.

"He has a knife, Kupki, be careful, call him monsieur."

"Look," said Kupki, "what the hell do you want?"

"Kupki," said Wozzeck, "he has a knife, a big knife, and all I've got is a roll of toilet paper."

"One more trick like that," said the Murderer, "and the two of you are dead men."

Then the door was opened and slammed shut. "He's gone," said Kupki.

"Did you see him?"

Suddenly the room was flooded with light. Wozzeck cautiously adjusted his trousers and peered around the partition. And all he could see was Kupki, quietly vomiting into the sink.

* * *

Wozzeck could still not put two and two together. Sometimes he came up with three and a half and sometimes the result was five, and twice he arrived at a hundred and six, especially when he brought the Murderer into his calculations. It boiled down to this, then: Wozzeck was working for a man in a gray suit and shades who seemed to head a company called UniRex. Then there was the matter of a murdered man in a métro station, a man in a blue suit with a mustache and open eyes. And now some lunatic was telling him to keep off the territory of one called Lunel, "Rocco Lunel," said the man in the gray suit when

Kupki and Wozzeck showed up the next day to make another delivery, "a well-known narcotics dealer. It appears someone had been holding a grudge against him. He was stabbed to death, as you well know, Monsieur Wozzeck, Monday night at the Gambetta station of the Paris métro. It seems the police are at their wits' end. They have a murder weapon and a set of fingerprints, but they still cannot locate the suspect. There are other people also interested in finding the man who committed this crime, people such as Lunel's family and the men who worked for him. It is fortunate for the assassin there were no witnesses, and yet it is equally unfortunate that some of us know exactly to whom the fingerprints on the knife belong."

They had arrived at the office at noon, two hours after Kupki had been contacted by another man in a gray suit and dark glasses. Rita had been waiting to greet them, giggling, happy Rita, who burst into laughter when she saw Wozzeck with his little headphones attached to his skull. He did not find Eric Dolphy's bass clarinet all that amusing, heartbreakingly wonderful perhaps, but not what you might call funny, either peculiar or ha-ha. And then she laughed again and compared Wozzeck to the late Chico Marx, and then without warning the man in the gray suit told this tale about a murdered man named Lunel, suddenly he felt he was being fingered, him, diminutive Wozzeck.

"What, you are saying I killed this man Lunel? I don't even know anyone called Lunel, why should I want to kill someone I've never even met? This does not make me at all happy," he went on, he was in a rage, "as a matter of fact it does not even give me the slightest thrill. No, no, never again, no more deliveries, no more UniRex, no more anything. I quit, kaputsky, *auf Wiedersehen*, bye-bye."

"But you cannot quit," the gray man said calmly and with a smile. And Rita too was smiling, blankly and unthinkingly as a beauty queen smiles, with her teeth and her body. "You cannot quit," the man went on, "because you have no grounds for doing so. If you murdered Lunel that does not unduly move us one way or the other. Clearly Monsieur Vezzani asked you to perform this task. It merely saves us the trouble of doing it ourselves."

"Yes, yes, that's fine, all very nice, but I've got a surprise for you, last night a strange man threatened to kill me if I didn't keep off Rocco Lunel's territory."

"Then you are perfectly safe," said the man as he lit up a cigar. "As long as no one outside this room knows of your little indiscretion you are out of harm's way. This man who you claim threatened you, I shouldn't worry too much about it. You see, UniRex is a large company, we dominate the competition. Therefore it is quite normal that others would be unhappy about our continuing success here in Paris. Threats are something we have all learned to live with."

Rita handed out vodka martinis and settled on the sofa and looked at Wozzeck. "So now you can relax," she said. "Today's delivery should make everyone happy."

"And if we decide not to make this delivery?" asked Wozzeck.

"You are not putting two and two together," said the man in the gray suit, "you are not coming up with four," and of course he had taken the words right out of Wozzeck's mouth, he had read his mind, music he could play, books he could read, but when it came to mathematics he was like a deaf man at the opera, nothing he had seen made any sense.

"Come," said Rita, "sit down next to Rita and drink your martini."

The man in the gray suit led Kupki out onto the balcony, the view was nothing to write home about.

"You have nothing to be afraid of," Rita said, laying a hand on Wozzeck's thigh. "We will look after you." She stared into his eyes. "Drink up." He swallowed it in one gulp.

"The ways of the world are funny," she said as she went to get the parcel.

* * *

This time it was a simple matter of meeting a man in the Place des Vosges, a man who would be waiting for them, who could easily be identified by his white suit, red carnation, and leather briefcase. Wozzeck and Kupki arrived twenty minutes early and sat on a bench in the deserted square. Jerzy switched on his Walkman and listened to Billie Holiday sing "God Bless the Child." He felt like weeping, it was so beautiful.

After a few minutes a man in a white suit sat beside them, sniffed his red carnation, took a pair of dark glasses from his pocket. Wozzeck switched off the music and looked at him.

The man said, "Lovely day."

"You think so?" said Wozzeck.

"Magnificent," added Kupki.

"You have something for me?"

Kupki passed the parcel to him. Wozzeck held out his hand. "Three thousand francs, please."

"In a moment." The man took out a small gold pocketknife (Why are there so many knives? Wozzeck wondered), cut the string, and began unwrapping the brown paper. Inside the cardboard box was a smaller box, made of some metal, very shiny. Without a word he reached into his pocket and handed the two men their money before disappearing down the rue des Francs Bourgeois.

"Drugs," said Wozzeck. "I knew it. This company of ours, this UniRex, is dealing smack."

"Perhaps you are mistaken," said Kupki.

"Yes, you are right, Philosopher, I am wrong, we are delivering foot powder, athlete's foot has become the new underground disease. Yes, yes, it is all very clear to me now, the stuff's been paid for in advance, we get a couple of thousand for the delivery, and nobody knows where it's come from."

"Then how do they pay for it?"

"Through the post, by way of a middleman, I don't know. Yes, yes, it is like a scene in a book, it is clear as day to me now."

They began walking back toward the Beaubourg. It was a hot day, the sun was like a furnace, even the tourists seemed to be going insane. They skirted around the Pompidou and bought ice creams from a man with bad teeth. Wozzeck took one lick and forced his on a passing American. "I am sick at heart," he said.

"Look, if you don't want to go on with this I suppose we can just quit."

Wozzeck laughed. "Quit? Oh man, be cool, you can never quit, you heard what the guy said. Once you get involved with people like that you can never find the exit, it is like the KGB. You really know how to pick them, don't you, my venerable philosopher friend."

"So now what do we do?"

Wozzeck shrugged. "Keep delivering until someone murders us in a toilet. It's not much of an end, but at least it takes away the pain of having to deal in shit."

"But I thought all jazz musicians were junkies."

Wozzeck had had enough of Kupki. He turned south on the Boulevard Sébastopol, crossed the Pont au Change, and eventually made his way to the rue de la Harpe. He bought a *France-Soir* and stood outside the cinema where Heidi worked. He read about the murder at Gambetta, about how puzzled the police were, because gangland heroes are never stabbed to death in the métro, Wozzeck suspected they were shot and stuffed into the trunks of old Renaults or else put into cement coffins and dropped into the river, or else machine-gunned while getting their hair cut, a bit too much off the back and sides, *ratatat.*

And although he could not work out all the details, he realized that he had been meant to see this dead man, this Lunel, that his fingerprints were on the knife, and that just to ensure his silence someone at UniRex had planned the whole thing. Lunel had been following him because someone had told Lunel that Wozzeck was moving in on his territory, and Lunel wanted to murder Wozzeck, but instead was in for the surprise of his life when someone got to him first. It still didn't make any sense, it was like the time he had watched *The Big Sleep* on television and someone had got the reels mixed up, and he had become increasingly distressed thinking he was going insane, or that someone had poisoned his popcorn, even Bogart didn't seem terribly sure why he was doing what he was doing, one had the distinct impression that afterward he was going to shoot the scriptwriter square in his back-space key. And yet he felt no happier about it when, a month later, he saw a revival of the film at a cinema and the reels were in the correct order and it still didn't make any sense, *policiers* rarely do.

He went inside the cinema and bought a ticket. Heidi led him to his seat. He made her sit on his knee for a few moments while he watched *The Nutty Professor*. The intellectuals occupying the other seats laughed uproariously and passed comments and took notes for their film journals. Wozzeck did not feel compelled to laugh, but he did take the opportunity to share a cuddle, just for a lark. Then he got up and went home.

He played the piano for two hours, and for two hours he was a free man. But at the end of two hours he wished he could have another martini, he seemed to be craving one, so he took the métro to Boulogne-Billancourt and went to visit Rita.

"Ah, Jerzy, I was not expecting you," she said brightly. "You made the delivery?"

"Oh yes."

"There were no problems?"

"No, no, no problems."

She stared at him. "Is there something you wanted?"

"A martini, please, very dry."

He sat on the sofa and waited for her to make the drink. When she returned he was standing by the window and gazing down at a small playground. Mothers with their children were enjoying their innocent years eighty feet below his misery. He finished his drink and asked for another. When Rita reappeared with the drink she was no longer wearing her dress, but rather a silk dressing gown, and when she bent over to place the drink on the table he could see she was naked beneath it, her breasts pressed heavily against the soft material.

"I know everything," he said.

"But what do you mean?"

"I know what you people deal in."

She looked at him for a moment, then said, "Ah."

"I want out."

"Now, you know that's impossible, Jerzy." She urged him to return to the sofa and then sat beside him. Her hand lingered along the inside of his left thigh. It was the touch of corruption, and although he wished to do otherwise, he felt that he could only yield to her, all his will had been drained out of him.

"Drink," she said.

She led him into the bedroom, where they seemed to be alone. She removed her dressing gown and revealed herself to him, and before he knew what was happening he was making love to her, making love and enjoying himself. And afterward, while he had another martini into which she had emptied yet another packet of the white substance, he realized that he had come to the West not to be free, not to become a great jazz musician, but rather to be corrupted by this great civilization, to enjoy the forbidden fruits that for some reason were not cultivated in Warsaw.

While they lay in bed, side by side, sipping doctored martinis, some men came in, men in gray suits and dark glasses, and it was decided then that Wozzeck and Kupki would be put on a salary, five thousand francs apiece per week. It was an offer, the men in gray smilingly clarified, that could not be refused. And it was then Wozzeck became aware of reality, and saw how sweet it was, the time had come to rejoice.

* * *

"I wish to give notice," he told Gino that night.

But Gino only laughed.

"I can no longer work for you."

"Listen, don't be stupid," said the Corsican.

"Nobody says no to Gino," announced one of his henchmen.

Wozzeck glanced at the pinups on the wall, he saw the bed with its crumpled sheets and blankets.

Gino smiled and rubbed his fingers slowly together, as if attempting to invent fire. "It's a question of money, then, eh?"

"No, no, I have no complaints on that subject," said the musician.

"So what does it come down to, you don't like Gino, is that it?"

"No, you are mistaken, Gino, I am your greatest fan, there is no one who likes you more. It is just that I have found other means of employment."

Gino rose, came around to the front of his desk, unbuttoned his jacket and looked down at small Wozzeck who, in turn, looked up at a large automatic pistol in its shoulder holster. "No one jilts Gino," he said, aiming a thumb at his chest.

Wozzeck said, "I beg of you not to take this personally, Gino, I have nothing against you. It is just that I no longer have the time to play piano in the evenings."

Gino looked at one of his men and then back at Wozzeck. "So who is it, eh? Carcano? Valenti? Giovanni di Angelis? It can't be that prick Lunel, he's dead. Come on, punk, who put you up to this, eh?"

"No one."

"What? I can't hear you."

"No one put me up to it, monsieur."

"So what is it, then?"

Wozzeck wondered what had happened to his wonderful imagination.

"Someone here stinks of death," said Gino as he returned to his chair.

"It is my wife," Wozzeck said.

"Your wife, eh. You knock her up?"

"No, no, it is very serious, we are all fearing the worst." He remembered hearing once how much hoodlums honored their mothers, there was no one greater in the world than the gangsters' mother, even Mafia warlords in New Jersey wept at the sight of them. "It is my wife's mother, we are all devoted to her. You see, last week she was run over by a car."

Gino looked at his cronies. "Yeah? So?"

"Isn't that enough? I mean, being hit by a car is bad enough, but to be run over, to have the wheels race over your body—man, that's not easy to take."

"So what does this have to do with your job?"

"I am so broken up that I am unable to play."

"All right, so you take a week off, big deal. Then you come back and play at Gino's club, okay, *d'accord?*"

"An excellent deal, truly a very generous arrangement on your part, Monsieur Vezzani, but there is something else. It was not a car that ran over her, it was a twenty-ton juggernaut, she insisted on taking her evening stroll along the highway."

Gino opened his hands. "Wait a minute, I don't understand any of this. You're talking about your wife's old mother, right? So what are you so broken up about?"

"That is an excellent question, Gino, if I may call you that, it is most perceptive of you to have thought of it. You see … my own mama died ten years ago, ever since then Heidi's mama has been like a mama to me. That is why I am broken up, it is like watching my own mama die again."

He hoped that God wasn't listening, for if He was He might just decide once and for all to teach Wozzeck a lesson and destroy these two women in a flash, it was best not to gamble with higher authorities.

"All right, so we give you two weeks off. That satisfy you?"

"Your generosity knows no bounds, Gino, there is truly something saintly about you, I knew it from the start. But there is something else. You see, we must go to Rome. Heidi's mama is a devout woman, she wishes only to see the Pope before she dies. It will be a long trip, perhaps even as much as a year or two, the old lady has every intention of walking there on her knees like a pilgrim."

"Mama mia, this guy is a nutcase," said Gino, throwing up his hands.

"In that you may be right, monsieur, you may have a good point there, your judgment is never far off the mark. I am almost embarrassed to tell you now the real reason why I must leave your employ. It is because I am insane."

Gino lit a cigar and smiled. "Go on." To one of his men he said: "Bring in the girls, I want them to hear this."

"Yes," said Wozzeck, his imagination flying out of control, "I am a desperately sick individual, the doctor has determined that I have fifteen distinct personalities, and still he is counting. This morning I was a Russian named Raskolnikov, my wife said I was giving her a splitting headache. An hour later I was the

Duke of Windsor, I was giving up my crown for the woman I love. Ah—I see you do not believe Wozzeck."

Gino slowly shook his head from side to side and cuddled a woman with gargantuan bosoms.

"All right. I shall tell you the truth. I can't play tonight, I am in no shape to do anything. I can't even see the keys, much less feel them."

"So you're sick, eh?"

"Only temporarily."

"You want a drink? Come on, boys, bring him a bottle."

"No, no, a drink would do no good."

Once again Gino opened his hands. "You want drugs, I've got drugs. Speed, coke, heroin—"

"Ah, I think you may have hit the nail right on the head, monsieur."

# 3

It was speed, then, no question. He had read all the available literature on the subject of drug addiction, mostly grim obituaries of jazz musicians, and had come to the conclusion that it wasn't heroin—smack, scag, H, horse, whatever—that he had suddenly fallen in love with, but rather a form of amphetamine crystal that made even a small man like himself feel like a first cousin to Tarzan of the Apes, he wanted only to swing from trees and ravish nubile Englishwomen, and afterward play the piano for seventy-two hours without a break.

You had, he remembered reading, something like two years to live.

Later that night, as he dragged himself home on the métro, Wozzeck realized that finally he had become like his hero Charlie Parker, the archetypal jazz musician, out of his head on dope and blowing his brains out, *toot-toot* to an early grave. And suddenly he no longer wanted to be a jazz musician, it was not much fun at all. He thought about what his mama had dreamt he would become and he could no longer imagine himself playing Mozart's 21st Piano Concerto, he would have raced through it even before the string section had the opportunity to have a last pee before taking their seats. He felt in his pocket and found the little envelope Gino had slipped him on his way out. He hid his face inside his leather jacket with the "Dizzy Gillespie for President" badge on it, it was worth a fortune, and sniffed the lot, and half an hour later was rejoicing in his existence, he was singing in the deserted streets, he feared no one, and when he came home he was laughing so hard that he even woke up Heidi's mama, who normally slept like a log, she had even missed the liberation of Berlin, not to mention the noisy arrival of the Russians.

Waiting for him, sitting in the living room and drinking tea and listening to Schubert, were Heidi, Ludmilla, and Kupki. They stared at Wozzeck as he removed his jacket and rubbed his sides with his hands. "So?" he said.

"Kupki has told us everything," said Heidi. "So you have been delivering drugs. Excellent. Hairnets I wouldn't have minded, there is nothing harmful in a hairnet or two. But for my husband to be getting involved in such a business is too much, Jerzy."

"And Kupki is so innocent?" he asked. "Oh man oh man oh man, that Kupki, my friend the philosopher, oh man is he fucked but good."

"Andrzej is no longer delivering drugs," said Ludmilla as she nibbled at a biscuit. Heidi's mama stood in the doorway, smoking a cigarette and smiling smugly to herself.

"Ah. I see. You think it is so simple?" asked Wozzeck.

"I won't show up for the next delivery, that's all."

"Too late, my friend, there is no way out. Mademoiselle Rita knows that we know that she knows—"

"And who is Mademoiselle Rita?" asked Heidi. "A woman, *ja?*"

"Look at your wife, Jerzy," said Ludmilla. "Look at her! Can't you see what you have done to the poor girl? Six days of Jerry Lewis and she is on the verge of a breakdown. Thank God next week it is something more sensible, isn't that so, Heidi?"

"This is so. They are showing a Clint Eastwood festival, I am going to buy myself a gun and blow out my husband's brains, that is what I am going to do!"

Ludmilla took Heidi in her arms and comforted her. "Shh," she said. Heidi's mother laughed quietly to herself.

"Is funny, yes, old woman?" said Wozzeck. "You think this is funny? Is it as funny as your last days in Hitler's bunker, you think so, yes? I am told you gave away the bride, your Aryan goddess, the late Eva Braun."

"Shut up!" screamed Heidi. "That is my mother, you bastard!"

"Oh yes?" said Wozzeck. "For a moment I thought it was Martin Bormann, already I see she has packed her bags and has booked a seat to Brazil."

It was half-past two. As far as Wozzeck was concerned, however, the night had barely begun. He paced the floor, rubbed his sides, licked his lips, and refused to yield the floor to anyone else.

"I am told Brazil is lovely this time of the year, you will go to cafés, old woman, and celebrate Hitler's birthday, there will be cake and beer and champagne and little cookies with the Führer's signature on them and then afterward you get to chew the rugs. What, you do not wish to go to Brazil? Very well, go back to Leipzig, you will find plenty of sympathetic people there, they await you with open arms, you will become a kind of figurehead to them. What, you are afraid of communists? Very well, monster, go to Paraguay, live in the jungle with the other Nazis, pick bananas with Mengele, swim among the piranha fish, I am told on good authority they are most loving creatures...."

* * *

When he awoke the next afternoon at one, he could remember nothing of what had taken place the previous night. All he could feel was a strange aching sensation at the base of his neck, as if his brain were being dragged down into his spinal cord, as if a shred of nightmare had become lodged in his nervous system, as if Fatty Arbuckle had climbed onto his shoulders with an armful of cement. He looked up, blink blink, shut his eyes. It seemed to him that he must still be sleeping, he must be in dreamland, for he could swear he had caught a glimpse not only of Heidi, but also Kupki, fat Bindler, Fetler, and a bewildered Blotnik. And it occurred to him that sometime in the night he must have died, that he was in his coffin, for there seemed no reason why Heidi should not be at work, or that all his friends should have gathered around him in such numbers. If this is death, he thought, it is not nice at all, I am aware of everything, soon I will see them nail down the lid and hear the dirt fall on my coffin and then I will be swallowed by the silence of the cemetery. And he wondered if he was to be buried in nearby Père Lachaise, and if all the dead people there like him were still in possession of their senses, in which case he would be able to pass the time exchanging pleasantries with the likes of Piaf and Proust and Chopin and Oscar Wilde, maybe death wasn't such a bad thing after all.

"He looks terrible," he heard Bindler say.

I should look good, a corpse?

"What has happened here, Heidi?" asked Fetler.

"Ach, don't ask."

They managed to get him onto his feet and to the kitchen table. Heidi put a glass of tea before him. "Drink," she said.

"I'm drinking." He was drinking.

"Eat." She held a spoon to his lips. "*Chlodnik*," she explained.

Afterward he felt like a new man, the pain was no longer with him, or rather it was no longer located in his body but instead in his soul, and he rather regretted the fact that someone had already written a tune with a title like that, for he could have played his own version but good.

"Today," Heidi said, "you go to your Mademoiselle Rita and tell her you're all finished working for her. Kupki has already decided to quit, isn't that so, Andrzej?"

"This is so," he said, as if participating in a show trial.

"He is turning over a new leaf, am I right?"

"He swears it is true," said Ludmilla.

Wozzeck opened his eyes and gazed at his friend's wife. She was wearing a tight blue T-shirt. It was summer, he was certain of it. He could see her plump breasts pressing against the cotton. He buried his teeth in a bun. "Oh man," he moaned.

"Take it from an old friend," said Bindler. "My best advice is not to get involved with these foreigners. Stick to your own and you can't go wrong."

"Is that so, Fritzi?" asked Wozzeck.

"*Ja*, it is sensible advice, it is what my beloved mama used to say."

"And what would she say if you turned down five thousand francs a week?"

"Five thousand francs?" exclaimed Bindler. "*Gott im Himmel* …"

He arrived at the apartment in Boulogne-Billancourt at half-past three and was greeted by Rita in a bikini. She had been sunning herself on the balcony. He gazed at her midriff and watched beads of perspiration roll down from her cavernous navel.

"Ah, Jerzy, I am so delighted you could make it today." She offered him a seat and stood before him, her legs parted slightly, she was magnificent and bronzed. "Somehow I knew you'd be back."

"I uh …" he began, "I can no longer work here, it is no good, no, it is impossible."

"What?" she said with a laugh. "But this must be a joke, we are all counting on you. Is it the money, isn't it enough?"

"No, no, I uh …"

She took her towel and began to dry her shoulders, and as she did so her bust bounced this way and that, it was almost too much to bear.

"I know," she said, perching on his knees, "I have been selfish, Rita has been a naughty girl, hasn't she."

He peered down into her deep cleavage as if hoping to find an appropriate response in the inviting darkness. But all he could hear was the profound silence of human desire. No, no, he thought, this time I have promised Heidi, I must not give in. "I am quitting, that is all," he said. "It is because of personal reasons that I can no longer work for you. Kupki agrees with me, he has severed all relations with UniRex."

Rita stood and went to make some drinks. He watched her as she poured something over the ice cubes. He admired the blue shade of her bikini bottom, it showed up very nicely her tanned legs, which were so long, so perfect, so smooth, like an image in a glossy magazine.

"Oh, I am so hot," she said as she handed him his drink and took a seat on the sofa. "Even in this tiny bathing suit I can feel the heat. Ah, that's better," she said, pressing her drink against her chest, making her nipples spring to attention.

"Oh man," said Wozzeck, setting down his glass. He could feel a battle raging within him, he could barely contain himself, he could think only of Heidi, who would always love him, he hoped. "I am going straight," he said. Rita giggled and leaned toward him.

"Then let's do something about it."

Afterward he decided it would be the last time he would do such a thing, it was a sin, there would be victims, misery would reign in the world of Wozzeck. "No, I am quitting, it has been nice knowing you, goodbye."

He got off the bed and began to get dressed, and as he pulled on his clothes a man in a gray suit and shades, who may have been the man he had met before, he couldn't be sure, came in and showed Wozzeck a video cassette, a film featuring Jerzy and Rita doing delicious unspeakable things to each other.

The man shrugged and took the cassette out of the recorder. "So what?" he said. "So you have cheated on your wife, that isn't such a big deal, now is it, Wozzeck? What really worries us is that you stabbed a man to death last week."

The man sat on the edge of the bed and smiled at Wozzeck. "Now, I'm sure you had good reason to do this. Perhaps you were frightened. I have often felt like killing someone who frightened me, it is a perfectly normal reaction. But you understand our problem, don't you? We could all be compromised because of what you did. We have placed all our trust in you, one of our finest and most efficient employees. Trust, Wozzeck: it is one of the most powerful words in any language, you understand me? We trust you, you trust us. It does not matter what the nature of our business is, for you are employed simply to deliver what we ask and then to collect your commission. So far it has gone well, has it not? I have heard no complaints about your work, not a word against you, my friend, and I see no reason why you shouldn't continue in our employ."

"It is not safe, dealing in drugs. It is also a little nasty, I think."

"Look upon us," the man continued as he led Wozzeck back into the living room, "as physicians. Our patients suffer from a common malaise, the world is hard for them to bear. They require, you see, weekly doses of medication. It helps them deal with reality more easily. Without these substances they would become outcasts, they might do some harm to themselves or others. Of course, each of them requires a different medicine, and so we try our best to satisfy their individual needs."

Wozzeck did not like the tone the man was adopting, it was too smooth, there was something dangerous underlying it, like a sheet of ice beneath the innocent drifts of snow, it was Warsaw all over again. He looked at Rita, who looked at him, and he could see it was a new look, a hard look, a cruel look, there was something obscene there.

"Kupki is no longer working for you," he said, quite by the way.

"What a pity," the man said. He took hold of the Walkman attached to Wozzeck's belt, gently unhooked it and held it in his hand. "Now, this is a nice little machine, is it not?"

Wozzeck thought it imperative he say something, anything. "The Japanese are most ingenious," he observed. "Inscrutable, small, and clever."

The man threw the Walkman on the floor with all his might and then ground his heel into the heart of the mechanism. "Clumsy of me," he said.

Wozzeck felt like crying, he had saved up for months to buy it, it had become a part of his body, like a second heart.

"Silly man," Rita said to the man, "you are always dropping things. A few weeks ago," she told Jerzy, "one of our employees was standing on the balcony. He went to shake his hand and the poor fellow tumbled right over the railing. He is very awkward sometimes."

The man took a box from the desk and handed it to Wozzeck. Inside it was another little stereo, a much more sophisticated version. The man said: "Just to prove to you our good faith. Yes, it was stupid of me to have been so careless with your little cassette player. But you see what I have done? I have replaced it with a much more expensive model. Go on, open it up, it's quite new."

"And it belongs to you, Jerzy," added Rita as she tousled his hair.

Wozzeck examined the little machine and remembered very well having admired this particular model in a shop window on the rue de Rivoli. He hooked it onto his belt and placed the headphones around his neck and wondered what the hitch was, to be given a present this elaborate probably demanded in return a desperate act, the murder of forty people or the nuclear destruction of Moscow, he could not wait to hear what it was to be. "Thank you," he said. He noticed that there was a cassette already in place. "This must be yours."

"Oh no," said the man. "It is a very special tape. I should like you to listen to it on your way home today. As for your friend Kupki," he said, rising and lighting a cigarette, "we are most disappointed in him. Such an intelligent young man, so handsome, so unmarked."

"But not as sexy as Chico Wozzeck," Rita said, dragging a finger along his cheek.

"It is a great pity," the man went on, "Kupki's wife works for Solidarity. Certain people here in Paris do not completely agree with that organization's philosophy. Of course, it is not so obvious that the cultural center is a front for a revolutionary group. These people I am acquainted with would pay handsomely to know of this, you see. They might decide to take certain measures against the employees of the center. As for your friend Monsieur Kupki, well, he is quite expendable, we only really need you, after all. That is why we initially approached him, you understand. To get to you. But Kupki could easily betray us, you see. Now, of course, Madame Kupki is a different story, she is an attractive woman, wouldn't you agree, Wozzeck?" The man stood behind him and brought his mouth close to Jerzy's ear. "Do you think often of Poland, my friend? Imagine what might happen if word reached the authorities' ears that you had murdered a man in the Paris métro."

"You are confusing me, I think."

"I have seen Madame Kupki myself," said Rita. "She is one magnificent woman."

"The last time a man tried to betray us we took certain measures against him. He too was married to a beautiful woman. After we finished with her she was no longer a beautiful woman."

Rita smiled and pinched Wozzeck's cheek.

"Think about it, Wozzeck," the man continued. "You are not a citizen of France, only a resident. All the police need to know is who stabbed Rocco Lunel. They will compare fingerprints. They may even talk of deporting you. That is, if Lunel's family doesn't get to you first. Do you know what it feels like to have your throat cut, my good friend? If not, I know for certain that Lunel's brother would be delighted to initiate you into this singular pleasure. The police too have their means of enlightening people. Oh yes, for a while you will be held up as a hero, you have killed a well-known narcotics dealer. But that will only be for the sake of the newspapers. Lunel has many friends in the police. They will wish to avenge his death. They too have many tricks up their sleeves, our brave gendarmes. There is an interesting little thing they can do to the eyeballs, I am told it never fails to make the suspect change his tune."

Suddenly Wozzeck did not feel at all well, it was as if a tremendous weight were pressing on his head, and he recognized a return of the old pain, the pain that spoke of an emptiness inside him. He rested his face in his hands and sighed. Rita massaged his neck and spoke soothingly of better times to come as the man prepared the syringe.

* * *

Afterward he felt much better. He was also five thousand francs richer, for he had given in, he made another delivery, it was on the way to the club anyway, no trouble at all. At the club he felt he was playing better than ever, the keys rolled under his fingers while tune after tune seemed to flow from the depths of his soul. He ended his first set with "Hit the Road, Jack," a great favorite the world over, and some members of the audience even put down their hamburgers and clapped their hands together, it was a great balm to his spirit, "*merci bien*," he said, "*merci beaucoup*."

During the break he was invited for a drink in Gino's office. Some of the men he often saw hanging out at the club, murderers and cutthroats the lot of them, were sitting around, dandling women in g-strings and spangled brassieres.

"*Bellissimo*," said Gino, rising to shake his hand. "What'll you drink, Wozzeck, tequila, Marie Brizard, come on, name your poison."

"Beer," said Wozzeck.

"Beer it is." He opened the little refrigerator behind his desk and presented Wozzeck with a bottle of Stella Artois.

"So you play the piano, eh?" one of the men said.

"Yes, monsieur, sometimes this is true."

"Hey, he's funny too, eh?" said Gino, picking his teeth with something that shone like gold. "Hey, Wozzeck, you want a girl?"

"No thank you, monsieur."

"What's the matter with you, you don't like my girls? Come on, have Maria, she's hot stuff, aren't you, Maria?"

Maria was the dark-haired one, very pretty and rather large, a great blowsy contrast to Heidi, who was blond and cool and lean, like a piano key. She rose from the lap of a fat man and strolled over to Wozzeck, engulfing his head between her breasts and making her tassels spin in two different directions all at the same time, it was a novelty act with a capital N, she was addling his brains. For a moment he could not breathe, he was suffocating on breast. "Thank you," he said, "that was most invigorating."

"Ha-ha," said Gino. "Hey, Pole, listen, I like you, you know that?"

"I like you too, Monsieur Vezzani, Gino."

"Good. I like it that you like me, otherwise I put my gun up your nose and blow out your sinuses. Let me show you something. Give me the book."

Maria opened his desk drawer and placed a leather photo album in front of him. He turned to the first page and pointed at the picture. "That's me, see. And you know who this is?"

Wozzeck looked. "No."

"That's Dean Martin. What do you think of that?"

"I think it is very nice, who is Dean Martin?"

"Ha-ha! Now look at this one. That's Belmondo. Once he came to my last joint, he loved it, he demanded to be photographed with me. Now put the book away, Maria." He gazed at her bottom as she opened the drawer and replaced the album. "Maria à go-go. That's what we call her around here, isn't that right?"

"Ha-ha," said Wozzeck, he did not like the direction things were taking.

"You on shit tonight?" Gino asked him.

"What?"

"Come on, you can be honest with Gino. You on shit?"

"I think so. No. What?"

"Still mainlining speed?"

Wozzeck moved his hand this way and that, indicating that it did not much matter one way or the other.

"What I want to know, see, is where you get your shit. I get my shit from the best people in Paris. They get their shit from the best people in Corsica, and they get *their* shit from the best people in Sicily. And you know where they get their shit?"

"Warsaw?" ventured Wozzeck, there was plenty of shit there.

"Laos."

"Ah."

"You ever go to school, Wozzeck?"

"Yes."

"You ever study geography?"

"Yes."

"You know where Laos is?"

Wozzeck shook his head.

"Neither do I. But they make the best shit there, the best shit on the planet. The top-of-the-line shit comes to me. The shitty shit goes to America, they haven't learned how to discriminate, all shit seems like Coke to them, anyway. Hey Rico!" he shouted, even though his brother was sitting not two feet away from him. "Listen, Rico, what's going on with the Lunel thing, eh?"

Rico shrugged and laughed, death was just another comedy turn.

"Listen, woe be unto him who stabbed Rocco Lunel. I hear there are at least six guys ready to slice him up if they ever find the guy. Me, I don't care, I never liked Lunel, that piece of infected shit. Oh, I feel bad for his family, of course I do, I mean his mother never hurt anybody, did she, Wozzeck, I mean she may be the nicest lady in the world, even though she hatched that prick Lunel, eh Wozzeck?"

Suddenly Wozzeck knew if he ever stepped out of line with UniRex he would be sliced up like a salami by six angry men who had worked for that shit Lunel with the nice mother.

"Look at this," said Gino, "I want to show you something." He removed his automatic pistol from his holster, it was enormous, Wozzeck began to pray. "This is a gun, see? From a range of fifty yards I can blow a man's head off, *ba-bouf*, just like this. From a range of twenty feet I can remove his hand, *ping*, just like that. You like guns?"

"So-so."

"What kind of a man are you that doesn't like guns?"

"It is just that I have never cultivated the habit."

"Listen, once I showed Dean Martin my gun, I said, 'Hey, Dino, you like guns?' He says, 'Sure I do, I'm a good American, I don't mind.' So I take out my gun and show it to him. You know what he did?"

"He showed you his."

"Ha-ha! He stuck up his hands, like this, see, right up in the air, I thought he was going to drop dead. 'I'm not going to shoot you, Dino baby,' I said, 'I only shoot people who get on my fucking nerves.' You know what he did?"

"Dropped dead?"

"Ha-ha! He sang six songs for me, just like that. Six songs and I didn't have to part with a centime, not a bloody centime."

"He sounds like a very generous man."

"Drink your beer, Wozzeck, here is another."

He passed a second bottle to Jerzy along with a small thin cigar. Maria found a lighter shaped like a urinating cherub and ignited the thing. Wozzeck felt instantly sick, it was like smoking a turd you find on the street.

"So, who's your supplier, eh? Valenti, di Angelis, Nico the Algerian up in Belleville? No? Come on, you can tell Gino, I'm like a father to you, right?"

"Yes, I think this must be so."

"Look, this is how things look. The people I get my shit from here in Paris, these guys don't deal on the open market, see. They give me good deals, I get all my shit wholesale. But I've got stiff competition, right? And competition isn't good for business, not when you're dealing in shit. Tell me, Pole, you well-hung?"

"What?"

"Listen, I've got a thing so long, I can shut the door with it without even getting up from my chair."

A few of the girls began to laugh, he must have impaled them to the wall in the past, it was all a great joke.

"I once hit a guy with the thing, you know what happened? He went flying off his chair and had to have a pin placed in his hip. Now I don't bother anymore, I just use my gun."

"Less wear and tear," observed Wozzeck.

"Hey, I like this guy, you know that? I like him a lot. You like him, girls?"

The girls all seemed to find him to their taste.

"How about you, boys, you like him?"

"Sure, boss."

"Then tonight, just to be generous to my friend here, I won't shoot his head off. But tomorrow I will if he doesn't tell me who his dealer is."

Wozzeck realized he had finally reached the point of no return, he was pinned in on three sides, Lunel's boys, UniRex, now Gino Vezzani and his bag of tricks, he was a dead man before his time.

"Now go play your music, Wozzeck, and no funny business, you understand? Tomorrow you tell me everything or else *babouf*, they will find your head taking a long holiday from your body."

* * *

After a rather low-key second set Wozzeck fled from the club, swearing never to return. He was still up from his afternoon fix, up and running, and yet his mind seemed able to contain fear, it was a most curious phenomenon. On the métro he switched on his new Walkman, an Aiwa with Dolby and radio and a thousand other little extras, Wozzeck wondered if it also shot bullets and dispensed amphetamines and cooked pasta and the like, it could become the housewife's best friend. He listened for a few minutes to the silence, removed the cassette, saw that it wasn't Art Blakey and the Jazz Messengers, remembered what the man in the gray suit had said, decided to play it through. There were two distinct voices. The more familiar one said, "Ah, how good to see you again. You are well, I hope?"

*"Très bien, monsieur, et vous, ça va bien?"*

"I'm splendid. Good, good … No problems, then?"

"None at all."

"You made the delivery?"

A pause.

"You made the delivery, all went well?"

"Ah, no …"

"You did not make the delivery, then. That is what you are telling me?"

"I couldn't … It wasn't possible, you see. I—"

"No excuses. You did not make the delivery as requested. And yet you have the nerve to face me and admit this. Then there is some redeeming quality there after all."

"I am sorry …"

"You are sorry. So. Look at this, do you see what I have here?"

Silence.

"Answer me, damn it! Do you see this?"

"*Oui*, monsieur, it is a revolver."

"What, tears? You are an infant, then? Do you think I'd waste my ammunition on a small-time punk like you? I need you, I need men like you, I cannot afford to do without you. Now, you have placed me in a difficult position, you see. For the first time in two months you have acted against my orders, you have failed to make a delivery. This is not good public relations, you see. Somewhere out there is a man who at this moment is suffering, suffering and plotting revenge against me and my company. You think this is a proper way to conduct business? Hm? Answer me!"

"No, monsieur."

Pause.

"No indeed. And so you have placed me in a difficult position, you have earned me an enemy. This was your intention, perhaps?"

"No."

"You seem very certain. You are perhaps working for someone else here in Paris, di Angelis, or Valenti, or even Vezzani?"

"No, no ..."

"And I suppose the next time you will do your job like a good boy?"

"Yes, I swear it."

"Yet ... How can I be certain of it, how can I guarantee the quality of your work?"

"But you have my word, monsieur."

"Your word ... But yesterday you gave me your word that you would make the delivery. And did you make the delivery?"

"No," said the second man after a long pause.

"Rita," said the first man, "get me the electrical cables and the clips, the ones with the teeth."

Wozzeck switched off the machine and wiped the sweat from his brow. The roll of fifty hundred-franc notes made a painful bulge in his trouser pocket. He got off the train at Réaumur Sebastopol and took a seat on the platform. There was no need to hear any more of the tape, it was quite clear what was going to happen, it was like seeing a film after someone has told you the ending.

He wondered too if his life was going to be as predictable as the tape, if what he was now imagining would come to pass, and if all along the men in gray suits had planned it that way. Tears fell from his eyes as he thought of his mama back in Warsaw, and of Heidi, and of the small joys they had all shared. He wondered also if the men who were ruining his life, these men of UniRex, had ever been innocent children, and he found it impossible to envisage it, he saw only very small men in gray shorts carrying guns instead of rattles, soiling their diapers, murdering their nursemaids in cold blood.

He waited for his train …

And while he waited he played a little game, for his curiosity had got the better of him, he could no longer stand the suspense. He pressed the play button and stared at his watch. For exactly ten seconds he would listen to the tape.

"No, please," the second man was saying, he was truly afraid, there was vibrato galore in his voice.

"It is the only way I can be certain that next time—"

Wozzeck switched off the tape and stepped into the train.

He sat down and treated himself to a further ten seconds:

"Now take off your clothes."

"No, I beg of you, monsieur, I'll do anything—"

"It will only take a minute. Now remove your clothes.… That's fine.… Now the other leg.… Rita, would you be so kind as to fold these neatly for our friend here?"

"But of course. Oh, these are lovely trousers, are they a hundred percent cotton?"

"Now the underpants. Come along, I haven't got all day. Good. No need to be modest in this house, we're all mature people here. Good. Now please lie across my desk—"

Again he switched off the machine. He left the train and saw that he had forgotten to get off at Gambetta, he did not know where he was, it seemed an impossibility that he could have stepped onto another train, he knew Paris like the back of his hand. It took him a few minutes to realize he was at Gallieni, that he was in the no-man's-land of Bagnolet. He lit a cigarette and walked back to the métro, and twice was propositioned by middle-aged prostitutes whom he suspected were spies either for Gino or UniRex. Once again he waited for his train. And once again he switched on the tape.

"—you will not let me down. Ah, thank you, Rita. Now attach the red cable to this bit here.... Just relax, my friend, it will only take a moment, just a moment of your time. The gray cable goes here. We'll start with fifty. Indeed we can kill two birds with one stone and try to find out if he's working for any of the others. Now, Rita, if you please—"

Right, that is the end of the story, I can no longer listen, I shall turn over a new leaf, put this all behind me, destroy the tape—and of course he switched the machine on, just to hear the denouement.

"Arghh!" screamed the second man. Then there was silence.

"The neighbors might complain," suggested Rita.

"Put on the music, then," said the first man.

There was a brief pause, then the sound of Maria Callas singing "Divinités du Styx."

"Now," Wozzeck heard the first man say, "we'll go to five hundred volts."

* * *

First thing next morning Wozzeck dragged himself to Kupki and Ludmilla's apartment in Montparnasse, more precisely on the rue du Cherche Midi. They had lived there ever since arriving in France all those years ago, and Wozzeck did not much like visiting their place, it made his own look like the shithouse Kupki always said it was.

Ludmilla answered the door in her dressing gown. She clutched it tightly around her bosom and stared at him. "Where is Heidi?" she asked.

"It is the weekly cleaning day at the cinema, she is on her hands and knees looking for fingers and bullets. Where is Andrzej?"

"At the FNAC, the big bookshop on the rue de Rennes."

"What, you will not invite me in, Ludmilla?" He took a seat at the kitchen table while Ludmilla poured him a glass of tea. She sat down across from him and smoked her cigarette.

"I am not well," said Wozzeck, "life has not been too good to me lately."

"You're telling me. My God, you have made a mess of things. And you have corrupted my Andrzej too."

"But it was Kupki who first got me into this."

"Andrzej is a genius, he is a philosopher, he is a man of intellect, he does not join the underworld every day, you know."

"Last night," said Wozzeck, "I could not sleep a wink, I was lying there terrified next to Heidi."

"What, you are still making deliveries?"

"I cannot get out of it, they will kill me otherwise."

For a moment she seemed to forget it was Wozzeck who was sitting across from her, she opened her arms and let her dressing gown fall open, for a second he caught a glimpse of the top of her breasts. "Then go to the police," she suggested.

"That is impossible, these people I deal with have set me up, if I go to the police I am a dead man, they will roll out the guillotine and chop off my head, like Danton and Robespierre."

"Don't be ridiculous, Jerzy, there is no capital punishment in France."

"For me they will make special arrangements, there will be a command performance."

"I think you are crazy."

No, he did not feel well, not one bit, he felt like he was falling into a huge pit, the old pain was incredible, he did not know what he was doing. He rose from the table and strolled into the living room. Shelves of books, volumes of philosophy and the collected works of Thomas Mann, stared him in the face and seemed also to be saying that he was crazy, except that they were saying it in German. He walked into the bedroom and lay down on the unmade bed, he could smell Ludmilla all over it.

"What, you are lying on my bed?" she said as she appeared in the doorway.

"I am not well, Ludmilla, have pity on poor Wozzeck."

"What, you are going to be sick, you will vomit on my sheets?"

"Please make love to me, it is what I truly need. My God, I do not know what I am saying, forgive me, magnificent woman."

"You must be out of your mind, Jerzy."

"Let me at least see you naked, Ludmilla, for years I have wanted this."

"Go to hell."

"You wish to see me naked, then? I will be glad to accommodate you."

She sat on the bed next to him and looked into his eyes. "Look. Let me call the cinema and get Heidi to come here."

"No, no, I beg of you, do not do that, I already know what she looks like naked."

"She will take you home and call a doctor."

Wozzeck tried to get off the bed, and it was only with Ludmilla's aid that he was able to do so, and of course for a brief shining moment he was permitted a full view of her left breast, it took his breath away, it was glorious, like Mont Blanc in the moonlight, "One touch," he begged.

She covered herself and backed away from him. "You're insane."

"It will only take a minute, I won't even use my whole hand, just three fingers. Two, then?"

And then, suddenly, he was in the hallway outside the apartment, Ludmilla was bolting the door and propping chairs against it and perhaps even the dining-room table. He thought it very odd that for those few moments in Ludmilla's house he had lost control of his thoughts, he was saying things he would never have said, he might even have lost a good friend, dear Ludmilla.

He rode up and down the escalators at the bookshop before he found Kupki in the section devoted to health and fitness. Kupki did not at first notice Wozzeck, and Jerzy was amused to see his friend looking at erotic photographs in an encyclopedia devoted to deviant sexual behavior, he suspected it was a monstrous best seller throughout the universe. "Ah!" said Kupki, shutting the book and turning aside. "Wozzeck, what are you doing here?"

"I have come to talk to you, Kupki, you are in deep trouble, they are going to cut up Ludmilla."

"What, are you mad?" He led Wozzeck into a corner, under one of the hot spotlights that made your flesh sizzle, it was like torture. "Now what are you talking about?"

"The UniRex man, you know? He said if you didn't make deliveries he would tell the KGB all about Ludmilla, you dig?"

"The KGB? What are you, a novelist?"

"Look, the shop assistants are staring at us, they think we are plotting to steal the collected works of Balzac, let us go back and look at the dirty book you were drooling over, I have a weakness for lesbians."

So they leafed through the volume while Wozzeck recounted what the man in the gray suit had told him. "And he gave me a tape, see, ah, does Ludmilla have breasts like these, they are magnificent."

"Shut up and tell me, damn it."

They stepped onto the rue de Rennes and found a café on the Boulevard Montparnasse where Simone de Beauvoir was sitting surrounded by fifteen adoring people, men and women alike, even children, and while she simultaneously gave a lecture on Third World feminism and drank coffee and smoked cigarettes and reminisced about Sartre she was also working furiously on yet another book, or sketching caricatures on napkins, Wozzeck was not quite sure. He told Kupki the whole story, right from the beginning, and he could see his friend did not entirely believe him, he was thinking Wozzeck was stoned on speed and making it all up, "France is no longer safe for us," Jerzy concluded.

Kupki opened his hands. "I don't know what to think."

"This is not good," said Wozzeck. "Give these lunatics the benefit of the doubt and get the hell out of it. Yes," he said to the waiter, "more coffee and five more croissants, I am suddenly starving to death."

He debated whether or not to tell Kupki also about what Gino had said to him, that if he did not tell Gino whom he was working for he would suddenly find himself in Dzerzhinsky Square with four flat tires.

"So the choice is yours, man," he said. "Either you make the deliveries with me and keep your mouth shut, or one day you will wake up to discover that Ludmilla is taking a twenty-year holiday in Lubyanka Prison, it is all up to you."

Kupki looked at him. "I think you are full of shit," he said, leaving the café.

* * *

Things were going from bad to worse, he could see that immediately. The old pain was back but good, his brain was being dragged down into his intestines, he walked the streets of Montparnasse and listened to France-Musique on his Walkman, a piece by Berg, very catchy.

He began to have the curious feeling he was being followed. He stepped into a secondhand bookshop on the rue de la Gaîté and for a few moments he felt safe, he was alone with the owner, an elderly man with a white cat and a running nose. And indeed he did feel secure here as he leafed through a volume of Baudelaire, there was silence, there were books, he could stand still. The man had said only, "*Bonjour*, monsieur, sniff," and had left him to his own devices. Wozzeck thought the effects of his comedown, what the jazz magazines called his crash, were beginning to wear off, and he was quite happy reading Baudelaire until the cat looked at him sideways and in a whisper asked if he were working for Valenti or di Angelis, and that was when he decided to give up and leave the shop, even the inhabitants of the animal world were on to him.

He returned home, somehow. And after he had two glasses of vodka he sat at his piano, and for the first time in his life found he could not make any sense of the notes he was playing, and so for fifteen seconds he simply banged out chords and wept. There was a knock at the door, it was his neighbor Monsieur Somethingorother, Wozzeck did not know, they had never been formally introduced. And this Monsieur Unknown threatened him with his fists and the wrath of the New Right if he didn't stop banging out chords on his piano, he was just like all these damned foreigners, the man was saying, good-for-nothing and a drain on the system, racially impure and so forth. So Wozzeck simply sat and leafed through a jazz encyclopedia, and he wished it were a sex encyclopedia instead, suddenly Monk and Miles and the Prez didn't seem so appealing, not in the state he was in.

He wondered when they would finally get to Ludmilla and prove to Kupki once and for all that Wozzeck had been telling the truth, that the world had suddenly become dangerous, that behind every corner there was an ambush. He hoped they would not be too hard on Ludmilla, she was an intelligent and kind and beautiful woman, she did not deserve to be locked up and butchered by half-crazed Soviets.

Wozzeck slept.

When he awoke it was to the sound of a tapping at the door. It was winter, the sun had set early, he could hear people walking on the pavement outside, their footsteps lightly muffled in the thin layer of snow. Mama had made *tchernina* that afternoon, she had devoted hours to its preparation, it was one of his favorite dishes; Papa's too. What is it Pavel Kott had done at the printing works? Papa was telling a funny story about Pavel, he was one of Papa's mates, he was always getting into mischief, was Pavel.

There is a knock at the door now; dinner has come to an end. Mama asks who it could possibly be at this hour, everyone is home eating, are they expecting company? Papa says there is a man there who wishes to speak to him, a man he does not know, "Don't worry," he says with a wan smile, "I'll only be a few moments," he gets his hat and coat and glances briefly at them and turns his back and steps outside into the hallway....

Wozzeck opens his eyes; it is still daylight. It is summer. He can hear the sounds of the street, he hears the sound of someone knocking at the door and calling his name. He reminds himself that he is in London, in a place called Hampstead, I am either dreaming or I am dead, or perhaps there is a third possibility, he thinks, I am not dreaming and I am not dead. He decides this is perhaps the more accurate description, but not necessarily the best, he has reached the end of the road.

A silver Rolls-Royce moves briskly up the Finchley Road.

Two boys find the body of a Russian in Epping Forest. He has been there for some time, this Russian, his flesh has decomposed, that evening the boys will tell their story on the news, a lady from the BBC and a lady from Thames Television will interview them, a forensic scientist will examine the remains. Death by misadventure, it will eventually be concluded, and no one will know who killed this Russian.

A Chinese widow weeps and beats her breast, while her daughter prepares dim sum and rice soup for all the relations who have come to soothe her pain.

It had rained for part of the night and now the sun is out on Gayton Road, there is much rejoicing in the land. Intermittently Wozzeck has awakened from his memories, he feels as if he has been watching a film. Now he hears the milkman making his rounds in his infernal milk van. He hears the postman on his rounds, lugging about his infernal bills, he even hears the newspaper boy making his deliveries, bearing the weight of the scandal sheets, which will soon speak of a death in Hampstead, everyone will read about it after playing newspaper bingo. And within himself Wozzeck carries on a debate as to whether he ever had a choice, and he decides that his fate was firmly decided by the man in the gray suit back in Paris, and all the men who worked for him and who also wore gray suits and dark glasses and who had taken away his free will, that pot of gold so treasured in the West. The world of free enterprise had proved to be an illusory one, he can see it clearly now, and all those wonderful leaders, presidents, and prime ministers alike were tricking the simple folk of their lands. And he wonders if by chance he had been made to suffer just to show the members of the working class what could happen if they began to listen to jazz and set out on a path of their own choosing. It was not worth thinking about.

Not now.

Not anymore.

He continues to sit in the chair by the window, and he knows that if he does not get up soon he will be arrested for murder or else left to rot, he would starve to death and feed the rats of Hampstead who nightly vacated the Heath for the rich pickings of N.W.3.

He will wait, then, just as the man outside the door will wait. To wait was a good thing, for to wait was to hope, to give up was not so good. And as he waits—*da-dee, da-dum*—he sings quietly to himself, it is his song, he is trying to catch the thread of the past, to review it just once more, to find out where he had gone wrong. He recalls that day he found Kupki at the FNAC bookshop on the rue de Rennes, he was thinking about it, he remembers, just before he fell asleep and dreamt he was awake and eating *tchernina* and watching his father recede into the future.

He remembers having played the piano in his apartment in Paris. He remembers weeping. He also remembers that at one o'clock he had gone to Boulogne-Billancourt, although he did not feel up to dealing with the complexities of the métro system just at that moment. Besides, he was a rich man, a roll of banknotes was burning a hole in his pocket, it was no good hanging on to so much cash, someone might take it. So he got a taxi to take him to the apartment in Boulogne-Billancourt, the driver put his foot to the floor.

Rita seemed very pleased to see him, though she was not even half-naked. "Right on time," she said.

"I am in no shape to make deliveries today," he replied.

She took him into the bedroom and stripped off his clothes and helped him to feel better, it was one of the specialties of the house.

"I need a fix," he said afterward.

"There is no question about it," said a man in a gray suit and shades as he appeared out of nowhere. "We'd be delighted to accommodate you. I presume you listened to the tape?"

"Who are you?" asked Wozzeck.

"A friend," said the man, adjusting his dark glasses.

"Not the same man I spoke to before," said Jerzy.

"It doesn't matter. We are all more or less the same. There are many of us, we all serve the same master. You enjoyed the tape?"

"It was most exciting," Wozzeck said warily.

"It's music to our ears," said the man in the gray suit. "Mainstream, I suppose you jazz fanatics would call it."

"More like hard bop," suggested Wozzeck.

"And so you have decided to work full-time for us."

"I have a choice?"

The man rose and began to mix a cocktail for himself. "I'm afraid not," he said.

"May I have a fix, please?"

"Certainly," said Rita as she prepared the mixture.

"You noticed that I said full time. We of course know you also hold a job working at Gino Vezzani's nightclub on the Boulevard Saint Michel."

Wozzeck looked away as Rita slid the needle into the bulging vein in his left arm. "That's hip of you," he said. He was feeling much better, much much better, he was a million miles away, soaring through the ionosphere, sliding on the shortwave spectrum, and suddenly, as if he had been staring at a jigsaw puzzle for hours on end, everything seemed to fit together. "Oh man," he said. "Was Gino ever angry."

"Precisely what we hoped for. Has he ever asked you about your work for us?"

"Oh man, has he ever, you should have—"

"You have spoken in detail about our operation?"

"No, man, I'm as cool as can be, just trust Wozzeck, he—"

The man took a seat very near to him, his shades were only half an inch away from Wozzeck's. He smelled of cologne and tobacco, he seemed to be carved from ivory, his hands were pale and slim. Wozzeck did not know what to say to this phantom except, "Yes, I see it now, you want to get Gino."

"Exactly. Now tell me about Gino Vezzani."

"He's very well-hung, he claims he destroys men with his thing, it is most impressive, I suspect he is also something of a ladykiller."

"But he knows about your dependence on amphetamines."

"Oh yes, Gino knows everything, I think he is a Freemason."

"Even where you get your supply?"

"No, I have remained mute, I have not said a word, nothing has escaped from my lips on that subject, I am like the fabled Sphinx of Egypt."

"Yet," the man went on, setting down his drink, "he has asked you this."

Wozzeck looked at him. "Asked me what?"

"Where you get your drugs, of course."

"Oh man, he thinks some guy named Valenti or di Angelis or someone called Nico the Algerian is behind it. Man, I feel I could run twenty miles," he added, leaping to his feet.

"Sit down," snapped Rita. "Sit down and be quiet, you little gnome."

"This is fine, you have done well," said the man. "Now listen carefully. I want you to tell Gino that Valenti is your supplier. Don't be so easy about it, you understand. Let him work on you a bit, allow him to pry the information out of your brain."

"No, no, that is not such a good idea, besides being well-endowed he also carries a gun, prying would not be welcome."

"Just let him ask his questions. Then let it out, appear afraid. Tell him Valenti is your supplier. That will start a war between the two mobs. This would mean a great deal to us, Wozzeck, especially now that Lunel is out of the picture, we would be willing to reward you. You understand what I am saying?'

Wozzeck understood him only too well, and he saw too that this was the only way to remove pressure from him, Wozzeck, and in that lay his salvation, there was opportunity in the West after all.

"Your friend Kupki has been told what could happen if he does not cooperate?"

"Yes, I have told him, he is not pleased. This morning, in fact, while he was looking at full-color photographs of—"

"He understands what the consequences will be, then?"

"No, monsieur, I am afraid not. But I beg of you not to hurt Ludmilla, she is like a sister to me, she is a beautiful girl, I knew her back in Warsaw, she is most attractive. Attractive and intelligent, such a loss would be felt on three continents."

"Yet you see the problem, Wozzeck. If Kupki refuses to continue working for us, he might simply go to the police and tell them everything. That could mean trouble for all the directors and employees of UniRex. You follow me?"

Wozzeck nodded. That was not such a bad idea, after all, now that he thought about it. Kupki goes to the police, the police arrest the men in the gray suits and shades, the world is right again.

The man continued, "And then of course we would be compelled to tell them about the murder of Rocco Lunel in Gambetta station. You remember, Wozzeck, whose fingerprints are on that sword?"

"I thought it was a knife," said Wozzeck. "This is very bizarre."

"But you see the consequences...."

* * *

His first thoughts were for Heidi. She had been suffering terribly because of him, she deserved better.

"Tonight, before I go to the club, I am taking you to dinner," he announced, trying very hard to smile, even though

Mama was sitting at the table eating *pain au chocolat* and staring moodily at him.

"You mean it?" said Heidi, clapping her hands together. "You mean that everything is okay again?"

"Fine, fine, all is well, the world will not come to an end, not this week."

He followed her into the bedroom and watched her change into her best dress, which he had bought for her a year ago at an expensive shop in the Forum at Les Halles, a huge hole in the ground filled with expensive boutiques, highway robbers all. He lay on the bed and gazed at her as she removed her jeans and blouse. She was still as lean and pretty as she had been fifteen years earlier in Warsaw. Twelve years, rather, he could not remember so well anymore. And even though she spent her days in a darkened theater, surrounded by madmen and intellectuals, he saw she still retained a certain bloom to her skin, she was like velvet, you simply couldn't keep your hands off her.

They made love and afterward got dressed and took the métro to a Chinese restaurant in the Latin Quarter that Heidi's friend at the cinema, Michelle Lebost, had recommended. The food seemed most peculiar to Wozzeck, he had not seen the likes of it in his life.

Heidi studied the menu. "Michelle says the Go Bow Loon is excellent."

"And what is Go Bow Loon?"

"Michelle says it is excellent. Also the Hon Sue Yoke."

"Hon Sue Yoke."

"And she says especially not to miss the Moo Goo Gai Pan."

The waiter wrote it all dutifully on his pad, he was Chinese and thin.

Heidi was delighted to see that Wozzeck was going straight. "Yes," he said, "all of that is behind me, I am going to devote my energies to you and my music, in that particular order."

She grasped his hand. "I'm so pleased, Jerzy. You know, I have been thinking. I am getting a little tired of working at the cinema. Perhaps I might be able to get a job working for Ludmilla's boss at the cultural center."

He remembered what the man in the gray suit had said he would do to Ludmilla. "No, no, they would never hire you, you are not Polish. Germans are not permitted at Polish cultural centers."

"But Ludmilla said it might be all right."

"No, no, I beg of you, take a job elsewhere, work in the métro, clean streets, sell postcards at the Louvre, perhaps you can even get a job here in this restaurant, you can run the laundry, I don't know."

Nothing more was said about it, mostly because it suddenly occurred to Wozzeck that he had become a full-fledged speed addict. At first he had never wanted to eat or sleep, he raced around with a dry mouth. Now, however, he was ravenous and he could sleep, to boot, a sure sign he had succumbed to the deepest form of addiction. "Oh man," he yawned, staring at his empty plate.

After dinner they still had an hour to kill before Wozzeck's first set, and much to their surprise they ran into Fritzi Bindler looking at the remaindered books outside Gibert Jeune. Heidi went to browse through the huge color posters of Alain Delon and Jean-Paul Sartre while Wozzeck stared at his friend from Berlin. "What, you have finished *The Devil Wears a Figleaf?*"

"*Ja, ja*, two days ago. The ending was most unexpected. Unexpected and inevitable."

"Good, hand it over."

"*Nein, nein*, I loaned it to Blotnik."

"Oh my God in heaven, now I shall never see it again, you must buy me another this minute."

So Bindler, who had trouble parting even with five centimes, begrudgingly bought Wozzeck another copy of the book and then afterward disappeared into the quais, probably to drown himself for having spent a fraction of his fortune. And when Wozzeck descended to the ground floor and went out to tell Heidi how Bindler had suffered so to replace his book he discovered that his wife had disappeared, it was most strange.

He looked here there and everywhere, no Heidi, not a trace, and suddenly he had a splinter of fear in his heart, for in the distance he saw a man in a gray suit and shades, he was being followed, watched at all times, it was the beginning of the end, he could see that now.

He looked into the Seine and saw nothing, neither Bindler nor Heidi, and suddenly it was twenty minutes to eight, Gino was expecting him, and here he was, lonely and widowed and miserable. To go to the police would be a *faux pas* of the greatest magnitude, they would take his fingerprints and book him for the murder of a man in a blue suit, and even though the man in the blue suit had been a criminal of the worst kind they would afterward get their guillotine out of mothballs and slice off his head, he was a Pole, he deserved no better.

He walked over to the Boulevard Saint Michel and kicked a few McDonald's wrappers out of his way, and pushed aside a few American tourists, the ones with the berets. He went from shop to shop. "Have you seen my wife?" he asked, and "My wife, where is she?" And he gave detailed descriptions of Heidi, her height, hair color, length of leg and so on, and nobody had seen her, they thought him insane.

When he finally reached the club he saw Gino stepping out of a black Citroën, and he told Gino what had happened, and Gino invited him into his office, probably to show him his gun and Dean Martin snapshots.

"Ah, Jerzy," said Heidi as he entered the club. She was sitting at a table, waiting for him. "I thought you had already started off for work, I thought I would surprise you."

"No, no, you cannot stay here. Oh my God did you give me a fright, I almost wet my trousers...." He hugged and kissed her and once again suggested she take a walk, preferably to their apartment, for it was not safe in the club, not tonight, not ever. "It is not ladies' night," he explained. "Tomorrow is ladies' night, then you may come and watch me."

"But tomorrow is Sunday, it is your night off."

"So it is, and yet it is also ladies' night. Perhaps they think me unfit to entertain the ladies. Anyway, my darling, here is a kiss, and I shall see you later, much later, after I have gratified the gangsters and ridden in fear on the métro."

Heidi was not pleased, especially as she was so delighted that Wozzeck had bid farewell to crime and drugs. "But I want to see you play, I am so proud of my little Wozzeck."

"Please, I beg of you, it is one minute before seven-thirty, if I am not laying hands on the keys by then they will be furious, Gino keeps a bull in the cellar."

"All right," she said, looking up at him from her chair. "Perhaps I'll walk over to Ludmilla's."

"Excellent idea, brilliant. Here is a peck on the cheek, goodbye."

"Wife trouble, eh?" Gino asked after Jerzy's first set.

"No, no."

The buxom half naked girls giggled, Wozzeck was becoming a nightly amusement for them.

"I mean, if she's fucking up your life, Wozzeck, I can take care of her for you, I can fuck up hers."

"Please do not trouble yourself."

"Sit down, Pole, have a drink. Beer, right?"

"Yes, that would be fine, most refreshing, beer."

"Your wife is a good-looking woman. She Polish too?"

"No, no, she is German, but a good German, not a Nazi."

"Ha-ha!"

"Ha-ha!" echoed his cronies and their molls.

"She is very amorous, that is why she did not wish to leave tonight. It is hard for her to tear herself from me, I think it is a case of animal magnetism."

"She a nymph?"

Wozzeck was not acquainted with the term. "Yes, indeed I think you have hit the nail on the head, a nymph she is, a German nymph."

"And I suppose you're a stud?"

"What is stud?"

"I'm a stud," said Gino as he unwrapped a cigar and slowly ran his tongue along the length of it. "Now last night you and I had a little conversation. Do you remember the topics we covered?"

"Ah, let me see. Dean Martin, no?"

"Yes. And?"

"The size of your genital organ."

"Correct. And?"

"Your gun."

"You mean this?" He reached inside his jacket and brandished the thing, waving it this way and that, he was terribly reckless with an instrument of death. "Last night Nico the Algerian was killed. Shot in the left ear. Someone even cut off his balls and stuffed them in his pocket. And do you know why?"

Wozzeck shook his head.

"Because he got in someone's way."

"Now he will not get in anyone's way, I think."

"Right. Now if you remember correctly, Wozzeck, I asked you to prepare an answer to a certain question. Do you remember what my question was?"

Wozzeck looked at the floor, at his hands, at his crotch, and wondered what Gino would do with poor Wozzeck's balls, they were truly dear to him, sometimes they came in handy. "You asked me who my supplier is."

"Bravo, Wozzeck, now we are cooking, as I once said to another guy who happened to get in my way in the kitchen." He reached inside his desk drawer and pulled out six five-hundred-franc notes. Then he snapped his fingers and Maria strolled over. She reached inside her brassiere and pulled out a small envelope of white powder, it was like a magic show, Wozzeck wondered where the rabbit was kept.

"Tell me who your supplier is, Wozzeck, and all this is yours. One ounce of the best speed in Paris and three thousand francs. This speed is so good that a speck of it on your fingernail will keep you flying for six or seven hours."

"It sounds like a remarkable product." He decided to play for time, he had an important decision to make. "May I have another beer, Gino, I am parched."

"Give him a beer," Gino said to Maria. He turned back to Wozzeck and fingered his pistol.

Wozzeck wondered whether he should do as the man in the gray suit had advised, tell Gino that Valenti was his supplier, or simply blow the whole city sky-high and tell Gino the truth. If he lied to Gino he would be castrated and killed, not, he hoped, in that order, and if he betrayed the men in the gray suits he would be tortured with electricity, it was hard to imagine what was the human race coming to, in his father's day they simply shot you in the back of the neck.

And then what would happen if he told Gino the truth, and Gino failed to believe him and decided to torture Jerzy just to get to the bottom of it, that would not be so good either.

He looked at the six banknotes and the packet of speed, it was an invitation to oblivion, he wished to God he could get out of it. He realized that many innocent lives depended on his answer, *his* life foremost, it was what was called in the Central

Committee a weighty decision, blood would flow no matter what. He thought of the people he was dealing with, Gino and his men, big stocky creatures who stood out in a crowd, men who moved their elbows when they strutted down the boulevard, cocks of the walk who could be spotted a mile off, well-hung men were such a rarity these days. And he thought of the men in gray suits and shades, there seemed to be more than one, he could not fail to recall *The Invasion of the Body Snatchers*, such a big hit when it was shown at Heidi's cinema some years ago. He tried to imagine what it would be like standing say on the rue de Rivoli, looking down through the arcades and seeing Gino's men, they were so conspicuous that one would run like hell. But men in gray suits and shades were not such a rarity, one saw them everywhere, they were conquering the earth like hordes of civil servants. So Valenti it was, then, let them battle it out among themselves, Wozzeck would quietly excuse himself and play his piano and try to go straight, anything was possible in this best of all possible words.

Valenti, he thought.

"UniRex," he said.

Gino opened his hands and looked at him. "UniRex? What is UniRex?"

"Let me think a minute."

"No, no, no, Wozzeck, there is no time to think." He aimed his gun at the ceiling and sent a bullet into the rooms above him, the tenants there were in for a big surprise. Wozzeck's ears were ringing, he could hear nothing but *bonnggg*, he thought he had lost his hearing for good, and therefore his job at the club, blind jazz musicians were a dime a dozen, but deaf ones, oh man, you could circle the earth seventeen times and not find a single one. He gazed up the barrel of Gino's gun and once again saw Death staring him in the face, Death was Cyclops, one-eyed and phallic, utterly Ginoesque in its essential nature, Kupki could write ten monographs on this one, he thought. So quite willingly and with a certain alacrity he supplied Gino with the address of the UniRex company, told him that Mademoiselle Rita worked for them, and spoke too of his deliveries and the excellent dry martinis which had led him into a life of crime.

"And now," he said, "let me have my speed and three thousand francs and I will keep out of your way, Monsieur Vezzani."

"Not so fast, Wozzeck."

Gino snapped his fingers, and before you could sing the first two notes of "Bags' Groove" there were machine guns everywhere, machine guns and boxes of ammunition, it was the roaring twenties, he could think only of *The Saint Valentine's Day Massacre*, a bloody and unhappy film about the underbelly of America's south side. In his mind's eye he could see Rita doing a danse macabre as the bullets riddled her body, he could see the gray-suited men with holes in them.

Before he left, Gino said: "Play your second set, Pole, and get out of here. Listen, you say one word about this and I'll personally track you down and cut your throat."

"In that case I shall say nothing."

"And if this UniRex turns out to be a joke I'll hold you responsible for it. I'm going to flush your head down the toilet."

And Wozzeck, inveterate flusher of rotten cabbage, wondered if they were now doing that too, back in Warsaw.

# 4

LUDMILLA WAS TOO TERRIFIED TO GO OUT THAT EVENING, even with her best friend Heidi. It seemed that earlier that day there had been some trouble at the cultural center. "It was all very quiet," she told Heidi as they sat in her kitchen, sipping hot tea and feeling their flesh creep with fear. "Irina was in one of her moods, you know what she's like, I've told you before. Men, men, men, all she does is complain. Today for the hundredth time she asked me if I was married, of course I said yes, and the next thing I know she is telling me to castrate Andrzej. So I play along with her, she is the boss, I say, 'How should I go about doing it?' and she says the next time he is raping me I should reach down and pull off his testicles, just like that, with my fingers."

"Irina Lapicki sounds like a woman with problems," observed Heidi.

"You're telling me," said Ludmilla, clutching her dressing gown to her chest. "But that's not the end of it."

"Perhaps she has no one to love," interrupted Heidi.

"You have made me lose my train of thought."

"I am sorry."

Kupki strolled in and poured himself a glass of vodka. He stood by the refrigerator and listened, for the second time that evening, to the tale of terror.

"There was this man," Ludmilla resumed, "a man I'd never seen before."

"Was he Polish?" asked Heidi.

"That's the funny thing. I could tell at once he wasn't."

"Ah. My wife the psychic."

"Oh, go back to your book, Andrzej."

He returned to the living room and sat in his chair.

"He was wearing a gray suit and dark glasses," said Ludmilla.

Suddenly Kupki was back in the kitchen, putting on his tweed jacket with the suede elbow patches. "Right, we are leaving, it is no longer safe here, I have suddenly put two and two together."

"What are you talking about?" said Ludmilla. "I haven't finished telling Heidi about what happened."

And he told them what Wozzeck had said to him, that the men in the gray suits and shades would inform on Ludmilla if Andrzej did not continue with his deliveries.

Now it was time for Heidi to do a few sums as well, for it occurred to her that if the gray men would do that to Ludmilla, tell the KGB about her work for Solidarity and so forth, they must have bigger plans for Heidi and Wozzeck, perhaps they would even bring in the CIA as well, just to make things interesting.

So for two hours they walked the well-lighted pavements of the Champs-Elysées and stopped for ice cream at Le Drugstore and considered their options, there being, in the end, only one.

Meanwhile Wozzeck was blowing the opportunity of a lifetime, Gino and his boys had gone off to a massacre and here he was alone, facing an expectant audience, he could play block chords, pieces by Bud Powell and Cecil Taylor, he could bang out his own "Meditations on Six Bars by Monk," he could even set fire to the piano and yet all he could think about was death, his own, it would be the great tragedy of his life. He played

"Strangers in the Night" for the second time that evening, and while he played he noticed that a powder blue Cadillac had pulled up outside the club, it was a car that stood out in Paris, a monster of a vehicle, an impossible thing to control that terrorized the boulevards and ring roads and drove innocent people into a state of mortal fear. And because the waiters at the club were by nature suspicious, because they, like Wozzeck, had seen one too many gangster films, they laid aside their trays and fled out the back, as did Wozzeck when he saw that the man looking at him from the front seat was wearing dark glasses and what he guessed was a gray suit.

He did not know whether to return home or go straight to Kupki's, he no longer knew what was safe. As he walked rapidly up the Boul' Mich' he could think only of Laurence Olivier asking Dustin Hoffman if it was safe, and of course Dustin Hoffman was in Wozzeck's position, except that Wozzeck was not earning twenty million dollars to act out a man in fear, he did not know what was safe, who was safe, where was safe, and so of course Olivier simply drilled holes in the actor's mouth, he was a Nazi, it was what they were trained to do to rich young millionaire thespians in the New World. He passed gendarmes on the lookout for terrorists, and Sûreté men eyeing swarthy Middle Eastern types, and Jerzy wondered if anyone would be interested in his case, he was condemned to death, he, an individual, a man with a past who loved his mama and his wife and his friends, a man who wept at others' misfortunes and laughed at others' terrible jokes. He was a man with a name, a face, human feelings, a man who dreamt of better things, a man who meant no one harm, a bebopper from the word go.

It was when he saw Heidi and Ludmilla and Kupki standing at the entrance to the métro that he knew things had gone from bad to worse, welcoming committees were like telegrams, they boded only ill. Ludmilla told him her tale about the gray-suited man in the dark glasses, Kupki apologized to him, there were kisses and embraces all around even though they knew that if they went home they would be walking into a deathtrap.

"Ludmilla and Kupki are coming to stay with us," said Heidi. She was looking at her husband peculiarly, as if she were not quite seeing the man she had married, looking as it were through his face onto the rear wall of his skull, there where the writing on the wall was, it spoke of drug addiction and crime and fear, and she knew then that her beloved was lost to her, lost forever, he was there but not quite there, he had entered the underworld and lived only among demons and ghosts, it was Warsaw all over again, "Oh my darling," she said, grasping onto him.

Tears came to his eyes. For the first time in his life he was at a loss for words.

* * *

Wozzeck knew he would have to return to the club, for if he didn't he would never receive his first-rate speed or his money, money which no longer much mattered to him, he did not want to be wealthy anymore, it counted for little in his world. But the speed he required to keep him alive, to ward off the crash and the old pain, to keep away nightmare and fear, to relieve the itch that tortured and the ache that killed. He knew he would also have to return to show that he was an honest man, to prove that UniRex was no joke, no laughing matter, that he was a man of his word and did not wish to be castrated by laughing Gino.

"We shall have to leave Paris," Kupki declared when they got home and sat down to talk things over, and Wozzeck thought it was the most sensible thing he had heard since Andrzej came to the club and said "Listen," which of course had led them to this point, one day he would pay for it. And everyone knew this was the only answer, leaving Paris, it was a great relief, it would have been even greater had they known where to go.

There was always Warsaw, of course, they all had lots of friends there, friends and relatives, their mamas, Uncle Stepan and his goiter, Auntie Irina, and of course Wozzeck knew they could count on the secret police to give them a bang-up welcome, it would be fireworks and *chlodnik* for the next thirty years.

"We could go to Leipzig for a few months, I suppose," suggested Heidi, forgetting that the secret police there had all sorts of tricks up their sleeves, they made their Polish counterparts seem like Boy Scouts.

"There is always London," said Kupki, and suddenly everyone knew this was the answer, for the first two suggestions were clearly straight out of the theater of the absurd. "My Uncle Pavel lives there," he went on. "Of course I haven't seen him in twenty years, but nevertheless he lives there."

"He will accommodate us?" asked Ludmilla.

"Of course not, he is as cheap as his brother Stepan, but I am sure he will put us up for a few days until things cool down here."

So for the next two hours they discussed the possibility of fleeing to London, secretly, in the night, under cover of darkness, it was just like wartime.

There was no question that they would have to leave Paris, Kupki was right. It was a matter Wozzeck considered as he lay beside Heidi and tried to sleep. He was but one small speck in the universe, he meant no one any harm, and yet this small speck was at the center of what appeared to be an intense battle for the possession of his soul. He could not quite understand why he, a nonentity to the entire world, was causing such trouble, jazz musicians by nature minded their own business. Had he committed some crime in his past, in his childhood, that had brought about this terrible business? He reviewed his life, or at least was about to, when he fell into a deep sleep. He dreamt.

He dreamt of his past, of what appeared to be the golden age of an ideal childhood, a childhood without politics or the secret police, an era blessed by the limits of home and hearth and Lydia Kovel's brassière, his mama sewing by the stove and a great fat black man who played trumpet like Rembrandt painted self-portraits. He dreamt of his early days with Heidi, this beautiful musician's daughter with her golden hair and brilliant smile, who laughed at his silly jokes and put up with his hopes for the future, who loved him and maybe now even pitied him a bit, small Wozzeck. And he wanted to weep even as he slept, for he had let her down, he had shattered the dream, Paris was no longer paradise.

And now he is returning from school, he is walking beside Kupki, he is talking about a musician named Louis while Andrzej kicks an empty cigarette pack from one foot to the other. They will stop for tea at Kupki's house and then Wozzeck will go home. Now his papa is sitting down to eat dinner with them, he is telling an amusing story about Pavel Kott, his mate at the printing works. Then the knock at the door, an innocent three taps, Papa is putting on his coat and felt hat, "I'll only be a moment," he is saying, and a moment stretches into an hour, a day, a month, fifteen years, the dream is slipping away, he is awake finally, ah Wozzeck, in London, in a Hampstead apartment belonging to a man he met only once, he is awake and in hell.

He speaks to the shadows, he asks "Why am I here?" and "What have I done?" and there is no answer forthcoming from the shadows, and worse there is no answer coming from within himself. He prays to God and begs forgiveness for his sins, forgiveness for the sins of the world, and yet he knows fate has guided him into this life, that this was to be his destiny, that fate has even worse rewards in store for him.

It is a beautiful morning in London. The sun is out, the rain has come to an end, people in the street speak of the Test Match and the inevitable decline of the Prime Minister, there is the laughter of young girls and the shouts of small boys, he wishes he could start all over again, he wonders why he was born.

Wozzeck prays for deliverance.

And once again he remembers....

* * *

Who has ever walked the streets of Paris, walked alone, hunted, and seen a black Citroën following him and not felt fear? And yet Jerzy Wozzeck could not be sure if what he was seeing was in truth a black Citroën, he had had so many hallucinations lately, he no longer knew what to believe.

And yet how alert he was, like a rabbit in the road. He had given up listening to his Walkman, it was a kind of aural isolation, he needed his wits about him at all times. Oh, music played in his head all right, it always did, tune after tune. Sometimes he was playing the tenor sax, blowing up a storm, bending and caressing the notes. And sometimes he was playing the drums, banging out his frustrations in complex rhythms, taking solos where none was called for, smashing his cymbals, seducing the blonde in the third row by tapping sexily on his high-hat, *tip-tap, tippitytap.* Sometimes he would play the bass, that great shapely instrument, full-hipped and buxom, and sometimes he would tickle her neck and people would faint because he had driven them all to the point of no return, it was such a pleasure to please the masses.

It was how he passed the time on the boulevards, it was how he got his mind off the old pain, it was also how he put off what he knew was the inevitable tragedy of his life.

Paris had shrunk. In a word. Smaller and smaller, *tip-tap, tip-tap* on the high-hat, *whoosh* on the snare, smaller and smaller, as if fingers were palpating the city, seeking out the malign tumor that was called Wozzeck. *Tip-tap, tippitytap,* he could hear it in his head as the Citroën advanced another inch into his field of vision, *tip-tap, tip-tap*, time was passing, and with every second that disappeared something of himself was diminished, this is the song of the condemned man.

He had betrayed his masters, they would most certainly punish him, there was no way out, *tippitytap, tippitytap*, "Ah, Wozzeck," said Gino as the door swung open and a gun was waved in a welcoming gesture, a graceful arc, a cowboy's *bonjour*. "Get in."

And Wozzeck had no choice, to be murdered in a car was perhaps better than being murdered in the street, at least there were no children to witness the traumatic event. He sat beside Gino, and the Citroën glided silently up the Boulevard Saint Germain. Gino gave him so to speak a guided tour of the vehicle, showed him the bar and the television and the telephone, and this last object was placed in Wozzeck's hand, he was invited to call his wife and bid her farewell, he was going to die.

"I don't know how I'm going to do it," said Gino. "But I'm working on it."

Wozzeck thought that flattery might work wonders with this man, and so he praised his car, its sleekness and beauty of line, its full array of optional features, he even speculated aloud on whether the car, besides being endowed with telephone and television and bar, also had a shower and a bidet and a working restaurant specializing in *cuisine minceur*, only a man as powerful and handsome and sexually magnetic could possibly deserve such a thing, not even Mitterand rated one.

"Watch this," said Gino. He pressed a button and suddenly on the television screen they were watching a strange little film starring three young unknowns, a man and a woman and a horse, and the man and the woman were naked and doing amazing lubricious things to one another and of course enjoying it, while the horse looked on and gnashed his teeth. "I even have a chainsaw," said the Corsican who was plotting Wozzeck's death.

When they got to the club Gino brought Wozzeck into his office and sat behind his desk, he got right to the point. "Listen, Gino is not stupid, we don't shoot first. We checked out this UniRex place you told us about. It would have been a lot easier if you'd said Valenti was your dealer, or di Angelis or even Nico the late Algerian. Then I would know how I would have to deal with them, they are recognized competitors. But UniRex, listen baby, you really pulled the wool over Gino's eyes, you fucking dead bastard."

Wozzeck was astonished to be hearing this, he had not done anything of the sort to Gino, and yet the shit was hitting the fan at a tremendous and deadly rate.

"I do not understand," he said.

"Oh yeah, we looked into it all right, this UniRex place. There's a girl living there—"

"Rita," said Wozzeck.

"Yeah, Rita. I hear she's hot stuff, Rita, a good-looking girl. How does the song go, eh? 'Rita the fucking meter maid'?"

"Something like that, I think."

"So Rita is UniRex, eh?"

"No, no, she only works for them."

"Well I spoke to my friends in the government and they did a little investigating for me and it seems that apartment is in Rita's name. Your Rita is a call girl with an income almost as big as my prick, Wozzeck. But as for UniRex, listen, there's no such company registered in France."

Suddenly Wozzeck knew Gino was about to do him in, he had to be convincing. So he told him the whole story, from the first words to the last, about the deliveries and Kupki and the gray men with no eyes, "and you see it seems to me, Monsieur Vezzani, that these people are clever people, not as clever as you, nor as alluring to women, nor as strong and brave, there is no question of that, monsieur, Rita's apartment is clearly a front for their activities, and so I would be grateful if you would spare my life just this once, I have troubles galore without having to worry about death right now."

Gino opened his hands. "I'm not going to hurt you, Wozzeck. Come on, Gino is a humanitarian, I give money to charities, I have important friends in the entertainment business. My reputation is golden. You think this dump is the center of my universe? You should see what I've got, travel agencies, dance halls, discos, a clothing import company, a Citroën dealership...."

And while he spoke he threw money and a little envelope at Wozzeck, it was an ounce of first-rate Parisian speed of the best vintage, a *cru* of the highest distinction, and Wozzeck scooped up a thumbnail's worth of it, and before you could say "Bird Lives" it disappeared up his right nostril and at once numbed his membranes, he could no longer taste or smell, what the hell.

"...twelve cafés, launderettes in Belleville, a prizefighter named Capriccio...."

And Wozzeck was flying high, he loved Gino, he loved what he stood for, he loved power and influence, he wanted to be corrupt and strong like Gino, he wished to be Mayor of Paris, what a novelty that would be.

"No, no, Wozzeck, I'm not going to hurt you. As a matter of fact I like you, I like you a lot, I think you're an honest man. So this is what I want you to do for me ..."

* * *

Yes, things were about to take a turn for the better, it was all becoming obvious to him. Naturally, he spoke candidly to Gino about his fears for the lives of his loved ones, Heidi and Kupki and Ludmilla and of course himself, that went without saying, and Gino was kind enough to suggest that when Wozzeck fulfilled his end of the bargain he should leave the country, London was an excellent idea, Gino had lots of friends in London, restaurateurs and murderers galore who would look after him.

He had three hours to kill before he was due to report to UniRex, and was relieved to have heard that Gino had not tipped them off that Wozzeck had betrayed the boys in gray, they suspected nothing. So he took the métro and went home, where Ludmilla and Andrzej had moved in anticipation of their trip to London.

"Heidi is at work," said Ludmilla. "Her mama has been looking after us."

"I have wired Uncle Pavel," said Kupki, "I have warned him that we are coming for a short visit."

"Oh man, everything is going to be fine, you will see," said Wozzeck. "I have made arrangements, there is nothing to worry about, leave everything up to me, we leave tomorrow."

And he ran around the apartment doing ninety different things in a matter of minutes, listened to Monk and Bud Powell records, practiced the piano, cooked himself some cabbage, changed his clothes, drenched himself in the shower, changed out of his wet clothes, discussed in detail the wartime record of his mother-in-law. "I am going to hold a tribunal the moment we get to London, she will have headphones and I will confiscate her cyanide tablets."

At four o'clock he was following his orders to a T, he was inside Rita's apartment, cool as an ice cube; although his temperature rose a bit, namely six hundred and seventy degrees, when he saw that there were three men there in gray suits and shades, one indistinguishable from the other, waiting for him, smoking cigars and admiring their manicures. "You have spoken to Gino?" one of them asked.

"Yes, yes, I have done just what you ordered me to do, I have told him that Valenti is the man, I do whatever I am told," it was like Nuremberg all over again.

"Excellent."

"And what did he say, what was his reaction?" another gray man asked.

"There is now a large hole in the ceiling of his office," said Wozzeck.

"Yet," said the third gray man, "we have received no signals about the expected war between these two gangs."

"Gino is not a man to act in haste. I have seen him at work, he is like Bernstein, Einstein rather, he ponders things, he weighs possibilities, he sets up hypotheses and tests them in his mind, he will come up with something clever, you will see, in three days Valenti and his boys will have disappeared from the face of the earth, the newspapers will have a field day with it."

"So you think that Gino will act before the end of the week."

"No question."

"Excellent," said one of the men, "now we can have lunch."

"Lunch," said Wozzeck as he looked at his watch, soon he would have to give the signal, he could not afford to work overtime. "But I have already eaten, many thanks anyway. I made myself a bowl of cabbage, it was most delicious, even though I am now experiencing intestinal thunderstorms."

"But you must dine with us, Jerzy," said Rita. "I've even set a place for you."

Wozzeck looked at the window. He knew very well who was down there, parked beyond the playground, he knew there were men there, supermen of the ilk of Gino, that they were waiting for his signal, there would be a massacre, doomsday would look like a situation comedy compared to what was about to happen.

"Perhaps I could make my delivery first and then dine with you. Yes, that would be an excellent idea. Allow me to fulfil my responsibility to you and then we can celebrate our success over liver and onions and vodka."

One of the men took his arm and led him to the table. "First we eat, then you make your delivery."

He sat at the table and was uncomfortable, first because his right trouser pocket was painfully loaded to the brim with the money he had earned from UniRex and the three thousand Gino had given him, and second because he did not like the drift of the conversation, he did not appreciate the way the tide was coming in, something was not cool here in Dante's Inferno. So he picked at his food, his caviar and toast and champagne, and all the time he could not take his eyes off the window, conversation was subdued. After a few minutes Rita got up and put a record on the gramophone, Callas singing "Divinités du Styx," it made his flesh creep.

* * *

We are well and truly at the fairground now, there are thrills and chills, ghost trains without exits and rides that whip you around like there's no tomorrow. Vagrants linger there, shady figures who stand by the shooting galleries and hungrily eye the boys as they step right up to blow down the ducks and win their girls a teddy bear. They meet, these men with their cheap cigarettes and disposable lighters, behind the fortune-telling tents, they have things to discuss, there will be mayhem at midnight.

It is a world turned upside down, this place where people sit and wait, it is strewn with rubbish, the ponds are polluted, bodies float beneath stone bridges, on the fringes of the fairground cars are aflame beneath a sky heavy with thunder.

And now we are on the roller coaster, for since that fateful moment when Kupki sat down and said to Wozzeck, "Listen," things have gone insanely out of control, the switch is jammed, there is no way out. And Gino is thinking as he smokes his cigar, he is thinking about Paris and the perimeters of power, he is considering the future and forgetting the past, he cares not a jot for this man or that woman, he wishes only to gather the reins of destruction and set off at a brisk gallop.

He will not wait much longer.

He is thinking along the same lines as the men in gray suits (and one of them says to Wozzeck, raising his voice slightly so as to be heard over "La Divina," "Ah, there is something electric in the air, I think we are in for a storm"), he is wondering if Wozzeck has lied to him, and instead of preparing to give the signal for devastation is secretly plotting against Gino and his boys; while the gray men are wondering if Wozzeck actually did tell Gino that Valenti was his supplier. But as these men are not men of trust, as human life is cheap to them, and there is no such thing as an honest soul, they may give Wozzeck the benefit of the doubt and do him in anyway.

They are watching the time, they are watching it carefully. Each minute brings them closer to Gino, each second is one less second in the life of Jerzy Wozzeck. Wozzeck will not be missed, gangs all over Paris know this. He is a Pole, his family was probably wiped out, he is an alien adrift in the big city, lost in the capitalist jungle, his death will not cause a ripple in the great sea of life.

One more minute has passed and Wozzeck is sipping champagne.

One more minute gone and Gino is growing impatient, the stink of betrayal is everywhere.

Rita, gray man, gray man, gray man, Wozzeck surveys them and fails to read their expressions as they eat their caviar and gaze contentedly at their honored guest.

Gino is checking his pistol, he snaps back the clip and hefts the instrument in his large hand and lights a cigarette.

Gino's boys are perspiring over their machine guns.

And although Wozzeck is trying to think about freedom in the London-to-be, attempting to play chords on the keyboard of his imagination, he can no longer do so, because he is now in the London-that-is, trying to fit the pieces together and wondering why he has survived, it would have been so much better otherwise.

The minutes pass. All he must do is step out onto the balcony, stretch his arms, breathe in the air of the city, that is the signal for Gino, we are at the dawn of Thermidor. He is trying to think clearly, his mind is racing, there are distractions, the music, Rita with her slim pale arms, the gray trio who play funeral marches instead of bebop.

"An excellent meal."

"I'm glad you're enjoying it, Wozzeck."

"Now before I leave to make my delivery I should like a breath of fresh air, yes, it will do me much good, I am slightly asthmatic," he said, puffing furiously on his Gitane.

"Come, what's your hurry?"

Wozzeck sensed that the gray men knew something was up, it is a most amazing phenomenon, ESP, one could make a killing at the roulette tables. He wondered too whether the men in the gray suits and Gino had combined forces, and if they had conferred the night before and just for fun decided to make an example of the dimunitive Pole with his big dreams. And he decided that all wicked men work together, serve one master, equally share the spoils of their crimes, he hoped they would realize he was simply not worth the trouble, at this, the moment when time will stop forever.

# 5

IT WOULD BE THE LUNCH THAT WOULD RETURN TO HAUNT him, he could not get it out of his mind. Part of the problem, of course, was that he was dining with three men with no eyes, or rather their eyes were hidden behind dark glasses, and he knew very well, having observed the secret police in Poland and watched the film called *The Comedians* with Elizabeth Taylor and her sweetheart and the demonic Tontons Macoute, that people whose eyes are hidden are people, dig, you cannot trust. Of course it didn't occur to him that he too was wearing shades, wicked mirrored things that sent back echoes to the bearers of ill tidings, and so the four of them offered laconic observations to their own images, it was like playing patience with a loaded deck.

Only Rita allowed her eyes to be seen, her big blue eyes, they were her best feature from the neck up, even though they offered him no hope.

As they were about to dip into their orange sorbet, Wozzeck broke the ice, "So you're going to kill me," he said, and there was laughter all around, great merriment, it was Christmas in July and don't forget it.

"No, no," said one of them, "don't even think about it."

"I am finding that difficult to do," said Jerzy.

"Your death is the last thing we want," one of the others said.

And Wozzeck was much relieved, he would not die in Boulogne-Billancourt, he would not oust Johnny Hallyday and Nathalie Baye from the headlines.

"It is funny you speak of death," one of the men said with a smile. "Most droll."

"I am told," said Wozzeck, "that I have a strange sense of humor. When I was a boy, back in Warsaw, my teachers found it slightly disturbing, they did not think I would make anything of my life. Ten minutes ago I would have agreed with them."

How they laughed! He was really awfully amusing, really and truly he was, they were eating out of the palm of his hand, Noël Coward would have fallen all over him, he was a riot.

"What is even funnier is that I am high as a kite on speed, I cannot even keep up with myself, in a moment I will ask you if it is tomorrow already."

"Ha-ha!"

"Ha-ha!"

"Ha-ha!"

Now that was most peculiar, it was not one of his wittiest observations, and yet these men were beside themselves, he could have pushed the lot of them out the window and into Gino's lap.

"Where did you get the speed, Jerzy?" Rita asked, and he knew then he had stepped into a trap, a great big one, full of poisoned bamboo stakes and tainted borscht, he would not easily get out of it.

"Gino, of course," said one of the men. "Who else, Valenti?"

The man was a born comedian, there was no question about it. Wozzeck smiled and licked the sorbet off his spoon, already he had spilled some on his lap, the orange spot would be a great embarrassment.

"It is funny you speak of death," his friend said.

"Have you seen the latest Clint Eastwood over at that cinema on the rue de la Harpe?" another asked. "It is a rhapsody on the subject, I give it five stars."

"Funny you mention that," said another, "I was at that movie a few nights ago. I took a fancy to one of the usherettes."

"Not the brunette with the big calves, surely."

"No, no, there is a blonde who works there, a blonde with short hair and long legs."

"Ah, I know," observed a gray man, "the one with short legs and long hair."

"No, no, you have got it all wrong. The one with short hair and long legs. I am thinking of asking her for a date. I pray she is into bondage."

"Is she available?"

"I hear she's recently been widowed."

And of course Wozzeck was following the conversation and enjoying every minute of it, he had had his reprieve, he was once again free. Yet a minute later, as he reviewed the repartee that had just reached his ears, he realized he had once again been condemned to death, that they were speaking of Heidi, they were going to tie her up and beat her to a pulp. But as he did not wish to reveal his discomfort and fear, he smiled and lifted his eyebrows and said, "Oh man, that's cool," and "I dig."

"It is funny you speak of death," came the chorus.

"Do you remember that fellow who used to work for us, that tall thin chap, the one from Antibes?"

"Don't tell me, let me guess."

"His name began with a *B*."

"Bardot?"

"Come, you can do it."

"Tell me more."

"He had a rare blood type, he said, it would be difficult for him to get a transfusion."

"It's coming back to me...."

"He also had a funny way of screaming. Oh, and remember how he shook when we pushed him into that hole in the ground?"

"Bonnet!"

"Excellent! You win the game, my friend. Yes, Bonnet, that was the fellow's name. A pity, really," he said, addressing his words to Wozzeck. "He had a great deal of potential, Bonnet, a brilliant future lay ahead of him. Too bad he spoiled it."

"Yes, yes," said Wozzeck. "Ah, it is getting a bit stuffy in here, I think I shall just step out onto the balcony for a breath of air."

"But you haven't finished your dessert, Jerzy," Rita said, laying a steady hand on his trembling arm.

"Gino is going to kill you," he said. "Gino and his boys are waiting outside in the black Citroën and they have submachine guns and they are going to kill you."

"Tell us more."

"And if I don't give them the signal I fear they are going to kill me instead, it will be *The Godfather* all over again, except worse, Gino will not win the Oscar, this is real life, I think."

"Go on."

"I am supposed to step out on the balcony and stretch and breathe in the air, and then they will rush the building, they will lay siege to this apartment, they will riddle your bodies with bullets, I assure you it will not be a pretty sight."

"Excellent, you have done well, Wozzeck."

"You understand that I am telling you this because I am a gentleman, I wish to be frank with you."

"What he is trying to say," interrupted Rita, "is that he has enjoyed his work with UniRex."

"Yes, that is it, Rita has put it very well, she is a born orator, I have enjoyed my job, I have found it a great challenge, I have come to consider you my own brothers, I would never let you down."

Rita poured the coffee.

"Yet you did not mention any of this when you first came in. I find that rather curious."

"It is funny you say that, lately I have been having difficulty remembering things, I think it is a genetic problem."

"But it seems odd that you would forget to inform your best friends about their impending death."

"As I said, messieurs, it is something I have inherited. My mother suffered terribly from the ailment, ten minutes after I was born she looked at me and wondered what the cat had dragged in."

This they did not find funny, the tone of camaraderie and hail-fellow well met had disappeared entirely, now things were becoming serious in the dead of a Parisian summer.

"Is it possible, Wozzeck, that you have gone over to the other side? Can we possibly believe, we whom you consider your own brothers, that you are now working for the Corsican?"

"That would be just too much to take," Rita said, staring at him. "We have been so good to Jerzy. Perhaps we should ring up one of Lunel's men."

"You have hurt Rita's feelings," said one of the men. "And Rita has been more than good to you. She has offered you her body."

"You are my lover, Jerzy, my only lover, our flesh is one."

"It is almost as if you and Rita were married."

"Please don't cry, Rita."

But Rita was not crying, she had turned cold as ice, she was auditioning for a Bela Lugosi extravaganza.

"Rita is my twin sister," said another of the men. "The last man who betrayed her was severely punished, now he no longer has the use of his limbs. For weeks Rita has been telling me how much in love with you she truly is. I have never seen my sister so taken with a man. And now … this? Come, Wozzeck, where are your manners?"

"Oh man," said Wozzeck. "Look, Gino is getting impatient, he is outside in a black Citroën, if I do not give the signal he will simply blow up the entire building, Paris will have yet another hole to fill up with boutiques. Please, I beg of you, let me just leave, I am not a warrior, I do not like guns, they make me nauseous."

One of the men walked to the window, hid behind the curtain, peered out into the road. "I see him," he said.

"How many are there?"

"Four, I think."

"Perhaps we could do a sniper job on him."

"No. Too risky. If it was just Vezzani, maybe … But with three others, no."

"We can kill Wozzeck and throw him over the balcony."

"A terrible idea," said Wozzeck, "I am terrified of heights."

But they had forgotten he was there, or rather he had become a corpse before his time, they no longer wished to deal with the living Wozzeck.

"If we do that," said Rita—his only love, talking like this?—"Gino might just get the idea that we mean business."

"We'll shoot him just once, between the eyes, and toss him out, okay?"

Wozzeck rested his face in his hands, he no longer knew where he was, why he was in nowhere and what he was going to do once he got out of it, which seemed unlikely now.

"Wait a minute," said Rita. "Why waste a good man like Wozzeck? He's told us a lot about Gino and his operation. He's a bum, a simple-minded jazz musician, he's one of the best people we've got."

"Please," said Wozzeck, "flattery goes right to my head."

"We can use him over and over again, not a single bloody person would suspect him."

"Yes, she is quite right, gentlemen, the lady is brilliant, one day she will qualify for the Nobel Prize in lifesaving."

"Rita's got a point there," one of the men said.

The one standing by the window did not agree. "I say we make an example of him. Gino thinks he's the biggest stud in Paris. Let's show him what we do to studs. We won't kill Wozzeck. We won't even waste our breath with Lunel's boys. We'll just cut off his balls and mail them to Gino. Then he'll get the picture."

"In that case," said Jerzy, "I beg of you, please just shoot me."

"I'll get the scissors."

Wozzeck appealed to Rita, he fell to his knees. "Please, I am begging you, please don't let them cut off my balls, what would my wife say, let them cut off my head, at least then I would not have to live with it."

"Shut up, you little Polish shit."

Wozzeck wiped the tears from his face with his sleeve and blew his nose on the Laura Ashley tablecloth, good manners no longer much counted for anything.

"I think we should discuss this a bit more," one of the more sensible of the trio said. "Rita may be right. Wozzeck won't betray us, not anymore. Maybe we should let him give the signal."

"You must be insane," said his friend who was going to operate on Wozzeck. "Gino and his boys will blow us apart."

"We have people all over the country we can count on."

"Yes, but they're not here now that we need them."

"Look," said Wozzeck, "I have an excellent idea. Gino will have to take the elevator to get to this apartment, dig? Why don't you just put a bomb in the thing, he will be blown to kingdom come, your troubles will be over."

They considered this for a moment, it was a good sign, his little voice in the wilderness was now being heard.

"Or we could be waiting for him in the elevator and then open fire when the door opens."

"And what do we do with Wozzeck?"

"Let him give the signal and then we'll see."

"Then we can push him off the balcony."

"Or we can take him in the elevator and send him into the line of fire."

"I thought I was a good employee, I thought you were going to need me in the future, I am most dependable, I will never let you down."

They turned their dark glasses on him. "You have already betrayed us once. How do we know you'll come back after we have killed Vezzani, where's our guarantee?"

"You have my word as a Pole, gentlemen."

"Ha-ha!"

"Look, call the Pope, he will vouch for me, I am his countryman."

"We can hold his wife hostage. Then he won't try anything funny."

In silence they schemed while Rita slowly stroked Jerzy's thigh. "Purr," she purred.

"Right," one of the men in gray suit and shades said. "Wozzeck gives the signal. We'll be waiting for Gino in the elevator." They turned to the musician: "Take the back stairs and get the hell out of here. If you aren't back by six—and I don't mean a minute later, you understand—we'll take your wife. And then we'll call Lunel's people."

The men went into the bedroom and collected their weapons, machine guns, and revolvers, gave Wozzeck the nod, went off to the elevator.

Wozzeck looked at Rita. "But where are the stairs?"

"Just get out there and give the signal."

"But how do I get out of here, where are the stairs?"

"Out in the hallway, you idiot. Now get out there and give Gino the signal. And if you aren't back here by six there'll be nothing more I can do for you."

Jerzy stood on the balcony and looked down at the Citroën. He raised his arms above his head and yawned, he was so overdramatic that he even would have lost the audition for Sade's little amateur production at Charenton, and he had seen the film six times. Four doors of the Citroën opened simultaneously.

"Afterward we'll kill the Pole," Gino was saying as he swung his legs onto the pavement.

* * *

"Right, we are going to London."

Kupki looked up at him from *Being and Nothingness*. "Now?"

"Yes, now, there is not a minute to waste. Where is Heidi?"

"She should be on her way back from the cinema," said Ludmilla.

"What happened this afternoon?" asked Kupki.

"Oh man, don't ask, I'll tell you later." He picked up the phone and made reservations for all of them, he was loaded with dough, up to his neck in fear, there was only one way out. "Old woman," he said to Heidi's mama, "you are packed, yes, you have gathered together your Nazi memorabilia?"

"But what's the rush?" asked Kupki. "Can't we go tomorrow as planned?"

"No, no, tomorrow would not be so good, I will be dead by then, a corpse is a heavy thing to lug to London, I assure you."

"But—"

"No excuses," said Wozzeck as he bade farewell to his jazz records, all three hundred of them; "no questions," as he gently touched his piano; "no complaints. We are going tonight and that is the end of it. They will be watching the airports, these monsters, we must take the train. Ah, Heidi, you are back, thank God."

"This Clint Eastwood festival is driving me insane," she said. "So much shooting, so much violence." Wozzeck could have died laughing, little did she know the facts of life. "What, we are going somewhere?"

"Pack your dresses and your lace panties and your Daniel Hechter blouses and your mother, we are going to London."

"But I haven't even given notice at the cinema."

"It doesn't matter."

"And we haven't said goodbye to Bindler and Fetler and Blotnik ..."

"That does not matter either, one minute wasted and we are dead ducks, the niceties of life do not exist in hell."

So they took the métro to the Gare du Nord and waited on the platform for the 6:50 to Boulogne. And although the Gare du Nord was crowded and noisy Wozzeck could hear only the silence of a city in which every third person could be your assassin. He stood by the little chocolate stand and waited for Heidi and Ludmilla and Kupki to return from buying cigarettes and Evian and sandwiches and magazines, Heidi was such an addict of *Marie Claire*. He remained close to Heidi's mama, gangsters would not shoot a man standing beside an old lady, and if things got tight he could always hide behind her, she was accustomed to pitched battles.

"Wozzeck," she muttered, "I am ashamed of you."

Wozzeck said nothing, his eyes moved this way and that, he was always on the lookout.

"What kind of a life is this? Do you think this is good for my little girl?"

"Heidi is my wife, mind your own business, troublemaker."

"And you are my only son."

"Ha!"

"That is how I look upon you. How could you have let things get this far?"

'That is an excellent question, perhaps you can provide me with an answer, oh Sybil of Stuttgart."

And suddenly it occurred to Wozzeck that Heidi's mama had put up with more than most people could normally bear, she had listened to his taunts day and night and had never struck back, she was a real trooper, storm or otherwise, she was no weakling who would claim she was only following orders.

He looked at her and saw age, history, a pretty young girl grown old, and because he had been seeing life in the raw lately he began to feel his heart soften, he wanted to make it all up to her. He put a hand on her shoulder and helped lift her from the bench, and restrained from making a joke about pushing her onto the tracks, *bouf*, just like that.

They got into the train, Heidi and Wozzeck and Mama and Kupki and Ludmilla, there were still fifteen minutes to go before it was to set off for Boulogne. Wozzeck and Kupki stood by the toilet and quietly conferred over cigarettes.

"How many people are after you?"

"Half of Paris," said Wozzeck.

"What happened?"

"Later," said Wozzeck, eyeing everyone who walked by them.

"Are you high?"

"Oh man, am I ever."

"Thirteen minutes left."

Wozzeck put his head out the window, he knew he was providing an excellent target in his flat-cap, he hoped it would be painless.

Ten minutes remained, and still nothing had happened, he hadn't seen a gray suit since Reagan's photograph on the cover of Heidi's *L'Express*, it was such a novelty. With relief he returned to Kupki's side and slouched against the wall, "Oh man," he said, "let's just get the hell out of here."

"I don't like this one bit," Ludmilla was saying to Heidi. "It's because of your husband that all this has happened."

Heidi said nothing and browsed through the bust-enlarging advertisements in her magazine.

"Oh, I know what you're going to say, Heidi, you're going to say that it was Andrzej who first heard about this racket, you're going to say that Jerzy was completely innocent, you're going to say—"

"Oh, do shut up," said Heidi, giving her friend a murderous look.

"Five minutes left," said Kupki. He had never seen his friend so nervous, he couldn't stand still, British tourists were looking at him with alarm, he would be the bane of London and the home counties.

"Oh man, this is just like a *film noir*," observed Wozzeck as he took a last look down the platform and the engine began to rumble and the sweat started to roll down his cheeks. And just as the whistle sounded and the train began to rumble even more, he could clearly hear the station public address announce: "Will Monsieur Jerzy Wozzeck please report to platform one." And just as he glanced once again down the platform, platform one, in fact, the very platform he was departing from, he saw a man in a gray suit and shades looking directly at him, for a moment he had thought he was safe, while all along he was slipping out of one bad story and, alas, straight into its sequel.

* * *

The journey to Boulogne was at first uneventful, long, and uncomfortable, obviously the SNCF had taken out their old wartime rolling stock for this journey alone, it was a kind of subtle revenge, the homeward-bound Britons would learn their lesson but good. All Wozzeck could think about was his lunch at Rita's apartment, he was beginning to feel as if he had gone to a film and that something had been left out, i.e., the final reel, and were he not a pianist he would have given his right arm to know precisely what had happened, whether Gino and his pals were now driving a hard bargain with the gatekeeper of hell, or whether it was the men in gray who were trying to dupe the deities of the underworld. And although it didn't matter which of them survived the battle, for they were all alike, the lot of them, Wozzeck began to relax a bit, for he was not being tracked from carriage to carriage by anonymous men in gray suits and dark glasses, no one had yet tried to push him off the train, and neither was he on the verge of discovering that the nun sitting three rows back was in reality Gino the Magnificent, armed to the gills and well-hung, in profound disguise.

In fact he slowly retreated into his previous life, he was a jazz musician again, he dug in his bag and pulled out one tape after another and listened to music on his Walkman and made funny faces and contorted his body as he jammed the night away; the other passengers, everyone an Englishman, finding him most amusing, now they would really have something to talk about when they got home.

Heidi was engrossed in her magazine, reading a succession of articles about marriage and divorce and tanning your breasts on the Côte d'Azur. In one of the other rags she had bought she read about the British royal family and how they all argued among themselves, on the links and in the field, there was talk about Prince Charles and his consort and how they fought in public, over foxes and grouse and in the opera house, it was most embarrassing to the Queen. And by the time the train stopped at Amiens to pick up some more passengers, among them a man in a gray suit and dark glasses, she was really fed up with all of them, the Prince and Johnny Hallyday and Gérard Depardieu, and so she put her newspaper aside and thus failed to notice a short piece about some gangster who had been murdered at Gambetta métro station weeks ago, and that it was rumored an East European with musical inclinations was responsible for it, there was a manhunt, all of France would not sleep until he was captured.

This was the *film noir*, then, this is how it would end, cinematically, on a train, the wheels clacking, muffling the screams.... The gray man would adjust his tie and take a seat and read Proust and travel on to Boulogne for his holiday, he would lie on the beach and dream about Rita, and then, because clever endings were all the rage, this had helped sell eighty thousand copies of *The Devil Wears a Figleaf*, Wozzeck would appear, treading through the sand, and exact his painful and humiliating revenge, a shade from the land of the dead....

"He is still there," Kupki said to the door of the toilet.

Wozzeck snorted another few crystals of speed, threw his head back, opened his mouth in a silent scream of ecstasy, and mopped his brow with a wet towel.

"Has he seen Heidi?"

"I'm not sure."

"Which way is he facing?"

"Ah, I am sorry, madame, this toilet is occupied."

Now Wozzeck knew he would have to emerge from his shelter, he had monopolized the toilet long enough.

"She's gone," whispered Kupki. He took a moment to learn the lay of the land. There were three cars, each equipped with a separate compartment where people left their bags and if they were in the mood went to relieve themselves or take dope in the toilet. The problem, of course, was that the compartments were separated from the rest of the car only by partitions of clear plastic, clear plastic and a door.

The coast was clear, Kupki opened the door and joined his friend in the toilet, even though there was no place to sit. "You are an idiot," said Wozzeck, "now we will not know if the guy is standing outside the door, waiting to do us in," *clicketyclack* went the wheels of the train.

"He is facing the other way."

"Can we jump off the train?" asked Wozzeck, before he remembered that they would all have to jump off the train, Wozzeck and Kupki and Ludmilla and Heidi and Heidi's mama, people would begin to notice something was up, old people do not abandon ship that easily.

"Perhaps," said Kupki, "we can make a deal with him."

"He's probably the one that wanted to cut off my balls, no deals."

"Now we are lost," said the philosopher.

*Clicketyclack* went the wheels in furious counterpoint.

Now the man in the gray suit and dark glasses was not in any rush, as a matter of fact he was reading the same magazine as Heidi, perusing the many and various photographs of Nathalie Baye, a beautiful woman, one day he would have to look her up, Johnny would not mind. He rose and strolled back toward the separate compartment, the compartment which was separated by clear plastic partitions, clear plastic and a door. He put his hand on the door to the toilet, he did not care that the sign said *occupé*, he did not give a shit, for when a gray man must use the toilet, he must use it, to hell with the occupant.

Wozzeck placed his hand across Kupki's mouth, his friend's philosophy was failing him in this moment of terror, *clicketyclack*, the door was being rattled and kicked, there was the possibility it had been constructed out of inferior materials, it might cave in at any moment.

"*Oui?*" said Wozzeck in the voice of a woman of a certain age, "*je fais pipi.*"

But the door continued to shake, the handle was about to fall off, and suddenly there was silence, now it was the man's turn to wait.

Kupki and Wozzeck looked at each other, their mouths were open, there were no words to express their horror. They thought of breaking the window in the toilet and throwing themselves out, Heidi and Ludmilla and Heidi's mama would join them later, they could help search for the mutilated bodies of the two men.

The man in the gray suit and dark glasses continued to wait, he had all the time in the world, as well as nothing to lose, there were men in gray suits all over the world, in high places and low, even in London, *clicketyclack*.

Wozzeck looked at his watch, and although he could have sworn an hour had passed since they had stopped at Amiens, only twenty-two minutes had gone by, twenty-two minutes of terror, it was like an advertising slogan for a Hitchcock film.

Six o'clock had come and gone long ago, six o'clock, the time of his scheduled meeting with the men in the gray suits in Paris, he wondered what they had had planned for him. Now it occurred to him that he and Kupki would have to get out, they were stomach-to-stomach, the temperature had risen to a hundred and ninety in the toilet, it was like greeting the sunrise on the moon, the ambiance was terrible. He began to whisper to Kupki, he spoke of leaving the toilet and disarming the gray man and then shooting him in the heart, after which he would be held accountable for the murders of two men, Rocco Lunel and a man in a gray suit, it was not such a good idea after all.

I am going to die, thought Wozzeck, there is no question about it, while Kupki was thinking the exact same thing, trying to console himself with the fact that eveyone was going to die eventually, so that it did not much matter if he died now, even at the tender age of thirty-eight. He wondered what would await him after death, he had his doubts like any philosopher worth his salt, and although until now he had opted for nothingness, he began to think that perhaps he was in for a big surprise, he would go to hell with Wozzeck.

Wozzeck was having similar notions, the heat in the little toilet was giving him ideas, he would die, and he prayed it would not take too long, he did not much like pain. He wondered if where he was going was a place reserved for jazz musicians, a kind of bebopper's paradise, if he would spend eternity taking lessons from Monk and sharing dirty stories with Mingus and comparing wingspans with Bird. The speed was giving him courage, he put his hand on the latch and pushed outward and suddenly he and Kupki were no longer alone, the man in the gray suit had decided to make it a threesome, he had joined them and locked the door, it was a tight fit and there was terror in the air, *clicketyclack*.

* * *

"You betrayed us, Wozzeck," said the gray man. Kupki was behind him, pressed faceward against the door, his hands were above his head, flesh against door, stick-'em-up style.

Wozzeck's shades were only half an inch from the gray man's, he could see dead bits of jelly behind smoked glass, it was the hour when the world turns a blind eye to murder.

"Gino is dead," he went on. "Vezzani and his boys are finished. Had you come back at six you would have been rewarded, Wozzeck, Rita was waiting for you."

"Yes?" stuttered Wozzeck, there was a parade of yeses, try to imagine it for yourself.

"And so you betrayed us," the man said, "and now you must pay the penalty. And I am delighted that your friend is here with us, for he must pay as well, he too has betrayed us."

"No, no, you are mistaken," said Kupki, even though his face was pressed against the door, it was beginning to get awkward. "I didn't—"

And then suddenly Kupki stopped talking, the man had done something to him, Wozzeck was terrified, terrified and sad that he had not had the opportunity to bid farewell to his friend.

"My friend is right," said Wozzeck, "a serious and possibly criminal error is in progress, my name is not Wozzeck, his name is not Kupki, you must have the wrong two people. Ah. I see you have not bought that one. How many of you are there on the train?" he asked, he thought if he talked the man might quickly become his friend, it was the only way to get to the heart of a murderer and terrorist, talk and flattery, it never failed.

"Just myself," said the man. "Of course there are others. In London. You are going to London, aren't you?"

"Ah, no, you have misread my intentions, even though you are an extraordinarily intelligent and handsome man with charisma, from a distance you are a dead ringer for Oliver Hardy. A thousand apologies, I mean Laurence Olivier. Kupki, you are alive?"

"At the moment your friend is unable to speak. In three minutes we are going to leave this toilet and go out into the area by the door. Your wife and her friend will hear nothing, they will see nothing, and by the time this train reaches Boulogne you will have become just another fond memory."

"But you are mistaken, my excellent friend, you have misunderstood my intentions, I had thought my appointment with you was for tomorrow at six, not today. We were on our way to Boulogne to visit my mother, she is dying, she is not expected to survive the night, all we wished was to say goodbye and then race back to Paris before six tomorrow. You must try to see it from my point of view, I have never enjoyed myself more working for you, I had every intention of returning, all I wished was to do the decent thing, a dying woman must be sent off in the grand style—"

"Shut up."

"*Oui*, monsieur, anything you say."

"Do you feel this?"

Wozzeck sensed something pressing against his belly, it was not a stethoscope. "Yes?"

"You will stay close to me, you understand? We will all leave this room together. We will make our way to the door. One word, Wozzeck, and I will kill your wife. Then I'll kill you."

"So you have made up your mind to do me in, yes, I can see that. There is nothing I can do to persuade you to do otherwise? Ah no, of course not, I am being silly. Perhaps if I explained something about myself, it is something I failed to mention to you at our meeting, but a number of very influential people, Mitterand and Jack Lang included, have been informed that we are traveling this route, they will become suspicious when we do not get off at Boulogne."

Silence.

"Ah. I see you do not believe me. Very well. Then I shall tell you the truth. It is no use killing me, it would only be most welcome on my part, you would be doing me a favor. You see, I suffer from a slow and excruciating disease, my life has been a nightmare, if you let me live I will be wracked with pain and remorse for the next fifty years, it is most unpleasant. Ah. Again I see I have not moved you. Kupki, you are alive?"

Silence, *clicketyclack*.

"May I make a confession, then? Of all the men I have dealt with at UniRex, you have been my favorite, I always thought you were head of the corporation, and if not then you deserve to be, you are a man of grace and good manners, strikingly handsome, you could pass for Dana Andrews in *The Best Years of Our Lives*. As a matter of fact, I have a treat for you. My Uncle Max is head of Twentieth Century Fox, I can arrange a screen test for you by the end of the week. Better, we can dispense with the test, he will cast you in his next picture, you will be a star, fifty million bucks are yours just for being yourself, there is a pressing need for the strong, silent type in Hollywood. Ah, I see you doubt my word. So. You are going to kill me, then."

"Anybody would, just to shut you up."

"Have you already killed my friend Kupki?"

The man shook his head, Wozzeck could see the reflection in his shades go this way and that, like at a tennis match.

"And yet you intend to kill him too, I suppose. A pity, really. Kupki is a brilliant man, he is also well-connected, his Cousin Tadeusz married royalty, a Mafia princess, her father is known as the Palermo Pulverizer, it is best not to mess with him. Now what are you doing?"

"I am opening the door. Just keep your mouth shut and walk quietly to the door of the carriage."

The heat in the toilet was incredible, everyone was soaked, even the toilet seat had begun to melt, the mirror was cracking, the soap was a travesty. *Clicketyclack* went the wheels of the train as they shuffled off into the corridor.

Wozzeck could see what the man had in his hand, it was a knife, he was going to cut their throats. The man put his hand on the latch and let the door swing open. A great rush of cool night air, a dark and soothing sea of black refreshment, engulfed them, Wozzeck could have stayed there all night. The man indicated that he and Kupki were to stand together, facing inward, near the edge. Suddenly the man hid his knife up his gray sleeve, all seven inches of gleaming stainless steel disappeared as Heidi's mama made her slow and laborious way toward the toilet. She stopped and looked at her son-in-law. "So. What are you doing here, you are up to no good again?"

Wozzeck grinned from ear to ear, just above the place where his throat would be slashed, "No, no, Mama, Andrzej and I are just having a little chat with our friend here. Ah. This is my mother-in-law. Mama, this is Monsieur Gris, no relation to the artist."

The man looked at her and then turned to Wozzeck. "Tell her to get out of here," he said.

"I don't understand you, Jerzy," she went on, "we were all perfectly comfortable in Paris, now you are dragging me to London, I no longer have the strength to put up with your pranks."

"Tell her to shut up and get out of here."

"My beloved Heidi is a bundle of nerves, you have been a terrible husband."

"Mama, the man wants you to leave, please just go to the toilet and get your business over with, just be quick about it, it is like a furnace in there, you will burn your backside but good."

She reached into her enormous vinyl handbag and withdrew a handkerchief, the tears were flowing, she was the spitting image of a Rhinemaiden in full flood. "You should only know what I had to put up with in the war," she wept.

"Oh, Christ," said the man.

"If it wasn't one thing it was another, then I have a daughter and she marries you, and suddenly my whole life is a nightmare from beginning to end."

"Mama, please, you are breaking my heart."

"One more minute of this and she goes too," said the man in the gray suit.

"Mama, if you do not make yourself scarce this man is going to murder you. Monsieur, I beg of you, spare this woman, she is an innocent bystander even though she has a dubious past."

The air raced through the open doors, the lights of small villages whizzed by in the darkness. "You make me sick!" Heidi's mama suddenly cried, lifting her handbag and swinging it with all her might, first it hit the man in gray, then caught Wozzeck on the side of his face. For a moment he lost his balance, nearly following the psychopath out the door, then he grabbed hold of Kupki's arm and righted himself. He noticed then that their party had been reduced by precisely one. "Where the hell is he?" he asked Kupki.

Kupki wondered how long it would be before they found what remained of the man's body beside the tracks. "I don't know," he said with a shrug. "First he was here, and then he wasn't."

They looked out into the galloping darkness of the French countryside, *clicketyclack* said the train.

* * *

It was after eleven when they arrived at Victoria Station, it was late and wet and they were starving, the train from Dover had carried no sustenance. To compound matters, none of them spoke much English, and Wozzeck saw he would not get much of anything on the little he knew, "dig" and "be cool" and "bebop" and "shoot the shit, man," and useful phrases like that, and so before they went off to find Kupki's Uncle Pavel they stopped at the little cafeteria in the railway station and proceeded to poison themselves on what seemed certain to be tainted food and tepid tea, it was enough to kill one's appetite forever.

They studied the map in the Underground and took the tube to Earl's Court and then walked a bit until they came to the house where Uncle Pavel was reputed to live, even though he hadn't responded to his nephew's cable. After they rang the bell for a while a blowsy woman answered the door, she was in no mood for foreigners, not at this hour, there was lightning in her eyes.

"You want someone here?" the lady asked Kupki. "One of the tenants, perhaps?"

"Ah, yes, yes, that is it, Uncle Pavel, just so."

"Pavel, you said, there's no Pavel here, at least I don't think there is. There might be a Pavel living with one of the others." She looked suspiciously at him. "He's not colored, is he?"

"Please?"

"Is he, you know, black?"

"Black? Please?"

She stared at him for a moment, blinked her eyes, smiled. "Oh, you must mean the old gentleman what passed away five years ago."

So they looked for a hotel, and of course London was full to the gills with tourists and terrorists and the like, there wasn't a room available, not for five people there wasn't. Then it occurred to Wozzeck that he was a rich man, there was no need for a cheap room, they could each have their own, with a private maid and butler and magnums of champagne and a concierge. He bought a map at a late-night newsstand and studied it with great care. "Here," he said. "This is where we will stay, I have heard of Piccadilly, they have a circus there, Heidi's mama can do a high-wire act without a net, most amusing."

They were refused entry to the Ritz simply on the basis of Wozzeck's appearance, he looked like a tramp, he had been through hell, there was worse to come, much worse. And so they managed to get rooms at a hotel on Half Moon Street, but only after an hour's negotiations, no one there spoke Polish or German or Russian or French (though three employees could muster up a bit of Mandarin), it was most distressing.

"Oh man, this is the life," said Wozzeck as he switched on the television and caught the last twelve minutes of *House of Wax*, Vincent Price was melting onto the floor, in Poland they would have scooped him up and turned him into six gross of candles. Heidi was soaking in a bubble bath, she had never seen so many bubbles, she felt like Marilyn Monroe before things had gone downhill. Even Mama had her own room, right next door, Wozzeck could hear her banging around and talking to herself, she was a magnificent woman, he would treat her to sauerbraten.

In the morning they ate breakfast in the dining room of the hotel, cold croissants and weak coffee and ersatz orange juice, it was like wartime, except that each of these feasts cost them five pounds apiece. They walked up and down Piccadilly, and Wozzeck proved to be a generous man, he bought Mama a silk scarf and a brooch, she had saved his life, she was deeply moved and also a little suspicious. And then, because he was a free man once again, he bought Kupki a Mont Blanc fountain pen and afterward they went to Harrods and let Ludmilla and Heidi run riot, he dropped a fortune in forty-three minutes.

Twice they passed newsstands where French papers were sold, he was tempted to buy all of them and read about the death of a gray-suited man with dark glasses, but that was all behind him, all he wanted now was to look to the future. And so the sun came out and they did some sightseeing, they went to Harvey Nichols and Buckingham Palace and Westminister Abbey, and all the time they did not see one man in a gray suit and shades, Wozzeck could have jumped for joy, even though it had begun to rain.

In the evening they went to see a play by Pinter, Kupki knew his work intimately in translation, and even though he could not understand a word of it Wozzeck shivered with fear, for something told him that this Pinter must have sometime in the past been on the wrong end of a deal with UniRex and had lived to tell his tale, it was a chilling experience, the audience clapped with joy and relief when it was over.

After they had been in the hotel almost a week it occurred to them that eventually, probably very soon, Wozzeck's money would run out, and so they would have to think about renting a couple of cheap apartments.

Heidi went to two or three cinemas to apply for a job, but as she did not know much more English than her husband, she was denied the opportunity to earn a few pennies on the side. Wozzeck too took a stroll through Soho, by the peep shows and nude bars and the Chinese restaurants with dead ducks hanging in the windows, it was most inviting, especially the flies that congregated around them. He stopped at Ronnie Scott's jazz club and seemed to understand that they did not need him, he stopped at sixteen other establishments, some of them of a very shady quality, and was told in much more clear terms that he was not required, and finally, to his surprise, he found a little place run by a middle-aged Russian, and within six minutes found himself employed, even though he was being paid less than were the teenagers who sewed sneakers in Taiwan. "I have a job at the Blue Pussycat Club," he told Heidi that evening, he could have died from joy.

Of course there were no apartments to be had, not in Mayfair at least, and they tried to translate all the ads and then went to a rental bureau where a pretty girl named Cathy spoke French to them and told them they could live in Tufnell Park if they didn't mind sharing a toilet with twelve other tenants, if they didn't much care that six of the tenants were ex-juvenile offenders with tattoos, and if it wouldn't be a bother paying almost as much as they were laying out in the hotel.

This did not seem a particularly inviting arrangement, and so she suggested some more apartments. Sometimes they would be living in a half-derelict building, and sometimes they would be in a very nice apartment indeed, save that it was unheated and devoid of fridge, shower, hot water, and bed. "But you can rent a telly," she said, as if that would solve their problems. "Of course," she added by way of a brainstorm, "you can come squat with me and my Mickey up in Hackney."

Heidi asked if Cathy could put them into an apartment that perhaps was slightly more expensive, a suite of rooms, even, that they could all share. Cathy thought about this for a moment and it was obvious she had found just the thing. So she put a call through to a man in Highgate and set up an appointment for them that evening, it was most exciting.

"We are going, you understand?" Kupki said to the desk clerk at the hotel.

"Oh, good. Very good."

Wozzeck listened to the tape he had bought that morning, a cassette that promised to teach English to people like himself: refugees and desperate Polish jazz pianists. "How are you?" he asked.

"Fine, thanks very much," said the woman at the desk, and Wozzeck felt like a million dollars, it was wonderful to be fluent in a foreign language. "I have a pain," he continued. "It is just here."

"I'm terribly sorry," said the woman.

"Would you like to have a drink with me? My name is and now you say your name, I am very pleased to meet you, I live just around the corner, please take my arm, I am in the mood for curry."

Kupki examined the bill as the woman pointed out to him the various extra expenses, taxes for this and taxes for that, room service charges and charges for using the telephone, television, bath, and beds. "Please?" said Kupki.

"I have a first-rate idea," repeated Wozzeck as the tape ran on. "First we will go to the museum, I understand there are many great paintings to see. Do you prefer nudes or landscapes? Then we will have dinner. Are you a vegetarian? Do you like pork? Would it be convenient to dine at a pub? I say, they do an excellent steak and kidney pie. Then we will go to the movies. I am not well. I have a pain. I think I may be ill. I think I have broken my arm, leg, neck, back. Please call me an ambulance, the fire brigade, the police, the embassy. Hello mate, hello cock, hello old boy. I have been robbed, oh man," he said, switching off his Walkman, "this is a laugh," even though he hadn't the slightest idea what he'd been saying.

Indeed, his euphoria was to last for at least two more days, forty-eight hours of joy and contentment and silly English phrases that didn't make any sense, but at the end of that time he was to realize that he had reached the bottom of the cul-de-sac, that life was short and art long, that there was no escape in this world, and that his story would most certainly have to come to an abrupt end.

# 6

BUT THIS IS ALL RATHER PREMATURE, WE ARE SPECULATING, Wozzeck has been endowed with as much free will as you or I, even though he has learned the lessons of history, he is a child of Poland, he expects only the worst. Faith? Who said faith? Oh, Wozzeck has faith, he believes in God, in salvation, he has even paid a visit to the Brompton Oratory and lit a candle and fallen to his knees and prayed to be released from the bondage of habit. To have faith in his fellow man, though, that is the great problem, he thinks of committees in Washington and committees in Moscow, committees made up of smiling bald men who sit around polished mahogany tables and drink mineral water and decide when the world will end, even though they nightly confront their people, the untidy masses, and promise a lifetime of sunrises.

But most of all he thinks of a man who knocks lightly at the door and asks you out for a moment's chat, for that is the most dangerous man of all....

And Wozzeck is right to be wary, he is right to fear for his life, and yet he does not know that at this very moment as they are moving into their apartment in Highgate, the Wozzecks and the Kupkis, as their landlord counts his lucre, there are men in gray suits sitting in Knightsbridge, and these men desire his soul.

UniRex has no central office, it works out of apartments and private houses and châteaux, for each employee in his gray suit and dark glasses is an entity unto himself, a portable corporation, and although each of these men was once a child, this one with red hair, that one with brown, though each has a different personality and varying tastes in wine and fish and music, they all serve the same end.

Now UniRex knows very well that Wozzeck is in England, they have suspected it all along and now they have confirmed it through their connections with the customs people, they have their hands in everyone's pockets. They fan out in twos and threes and sometimes singly, they roam the streets of London, they frequent low bars and opium dens, they have communicated with the narcotics tycoons, they have put out word that a man has betrayed them, that this man is a musician and a Pole, that he will pay for what he has done.

Now they are in Soho, they are peering through restaurant windows and paying their informers, they have combed the sex clubs and threatened the prostitutes, but they have not yet made their way to the Blue Pussycat Club, Wozzeck is playing up a storm.

"Play whatever you like," a middle-aged Russian named Makaroff had told Jerzy. "No one comes here to listen to music anyway. It is the girls they want, flesh and the devil, the world of jazz means nothing to them."

They sat and drank vodka in the back office, it was seedier even than Gino's club. Makaroff told his own story, the tale of his life, forgettable right from the start, Wozzeck knew it was a bundle of lies. "And so I made my way to Britain," he concluded, this Russian, and he related also how penniless he had been, dying of hunger, a man adrift in the West, forced to live by his wits, Wozzeck could not bring himself to shed a tear.

"But see how well I have done," he went on. "Ah, this club is maybe not what my papa had in mind when he told me to go out into the world and do good things for the human race, but it is a start, you do not agree?'

Wozzeck could not very well afford not to agree, he had a job, Makaroff was his boss, even though he had only a day or two left of his speed, desperation time was just around the corner, the old pain, the old misery, the lonely crash in a public toilet. And he knew that sooner or later he would have to connect, Soho seemed just the place.

And so he played his piano while men drank their beer and diluted whiskey and played with the women, and sometimes they would dance and sometimes disappear into rooms located along the sides, cubicles furnished with bare mattresses and towels, and they would emerge into the darkness of the night and blend in with the crowds, with their old friend Guilt, smiling and greedy, mincing alongside them.

The lights dim, the men drift away, the women change out of their cheap costumes and collect their wages and descend underground and rumble home, it is the end of another day. Wozzeck too, he must also leave, he shuts his piano and drinks some more vodka with Makaroff and goes home to the house just off Archway Road, the whole neighborhood smells of cooking oil and sides of beef, it is not quite paradise and yet one cannot complain, not even Heidi's mama, who has her own room with a view of the Hungry Friar, fish and chips sold by a defrocked Irish priest.

And so they slept, each family in its own room. Heidi lay beside Jerzy and dreamed about the Polish actor Zapaciewicz, he was such a hunk of a man, she thought she would die of passion. Kupki dreamed he was in a Warsaw slaughterhouse, the one his father had managed, and that Wittgenstein was sitting beside him dismembering a pig. Ludmilla dreamed about Wozzeck, it was most curious, terribly erotic, he had twelve fingers, each of them two feet long. While Heidi's mama dreamed about a man falling off a train, in twelve minutes she would wake up screaming, it was World War II all over again. And while they dreamed, each in his own world, Makaroff sat behind his desk and shivered with fear as the man in the gray suit spoke of a piano player and death and betrayal.

* * *

Now it struck Wozzeck as a happy coincidence that the next day, the very day when his speed was due to run out, Makaroff offered to give him some in lieu of part of his salary. "It suits you, then, this little arrangement?" asked the Russian, and of course Wozzeck was beside himself, he could not believe his luck; good health, a glowing future, and a thousand healthy children, it was what he wished for Makaroff, one could ask for no more, save perhaps a loving wife, a piano that was tuned more than once every twenty years, and a big bowl of *chlodnik*. And yet he did not feel he should tip his hand, not too much anyway, he still had not got the measure of Makaroff.

"So, you like it here in London?" he asked Wozzeck.

"Starting from two minutes ago, yes, it is not bad, I—"

"In Paris you played piano too?"

"Ach, don't ask, I played piano at this place run by a Corsican, now I cannot complain, he is dead and you are nothing like him, I hope. Oh man, this is the life," he said, fingering his little envelope of speed.

"I am glad you are happy," said Makaroff, he was a sneaky little Russian, he could not look straight at Wozzeck. "I am glad you are happy because that makes me happy, and when you and I are happy the girls are happy and consequently so are the customers. This is what makes up a happy world, do you not agree, Wozzeck?"

And this was said in so calculated a manner, with such sinister overtones, that Wozzeck instantly saw through the words, the man was not speaking about happiness, he was talking about betrayal and death, even though he was giving Wozzeck speed in place of part of his wages, one does not turn down an offer one cannot refuse, he had learned that lesson one too many times.

"Yes, yes," said Wozzeck, "I agree, worldwide happiness is a wonderful thing, the Pope has been pushing that line for years." And he could see straightaway that there was something different about Makaroff, something that was not evident before, as if someone were standing behind this Russian, pressing a gun between his shoulder blades, as if someone were listening to his every word, as if someone had it in for him, one could go on forever, the phrasebook of fear is most impressively rich. The tape he had bought was utterly useless, it taught an English that was not very current in this curious underworld, one did not go around Soho saying, "Please join me for a cup of tea," "Shall we head off for Henley, old boy?" "I came down from Cambridge in thirty-nine, do you remember Hoskins?" and suchlike, for here he needed a new vocabulary, a list of words and expressions penned with the point of a knife, here it was forever the sharp edge of night, the dead hour between darkness and dawn.

* * *

Language and gesture: what funny things they were, how much he had to learn in London. "It is curious," he told Heidi the next morning after taking his secret fix, he was twenty thousand leagues over the moon, "these English people seem to be as polite as my mama. Now the French, you remember the French, *n'est-ce pas?* They would just as soon stab you in the back before they would do you a good turn."

"I find the English very nice," said Heidi, though she had been unable to find a job and consequently spent much of her time squeezing veggies at Sainsbury's and buying underwear at Marks & Spencer. "People wait their turn on line, even the bus conductor helped me to get on," though she refrained from telling her husband that said bus conductor had also taken advantage of the moment to touch her backside, it was like an electrical shock.

"No, no, I am not so sure I am reading it all correctly, there is something funny about all these good manners, they have something up their sleeves, perhaps an Ace of Spades."

Kupki grinned to himself and drank his tea, he was finding London a most refreshing change, he had met an undergraduate from the London School of Economics who wished only to lie beneath him day and night, to commune in the profoundest manner with this intellectual from a troubled land.

So peace seemed to reign over the household with its separate rooms. But it was an uneasy peace, a suspicious peace, Wozzeck sensed it would all go sour, perhaps sooner than he expected, and when, lying awake that night and staring into the darkness, feeling the exaggerated *thump-thump* of his heartbeat as the speed flowed into it, he turned inward and sought solace, he instead found only an immense emptiness and the terrified echo of his own suspicious voice.

* * *

It was an Englishman in a gray suit and dark glasses who met him the next evening at the entrance to the Blue Pussycat Club. They went into Makaroff's office, Wozzeck had little choice in the matter, and of course Makaroff was not there, clearly they had done him the immense favor of relieving him not only of his livelihood but also his life.

"So, Wozzeck," the man in the gray suit said in French, "once again we have made contact."

Wozzeck looked puzzled, he smiled and opened his hands. "Wozzeck? No, no, you must have the wrong man, I am not Wozzeck, what a funny thing, perhaps I can help you find him, goodbye."

"Come, come, Wozzeck, we know who you are and, what is perhaps most dangerous of all, you know who we are."

"No, no, I have never seen you before in my life, I am not even looking at you, go away and I shall say nothing to anyone, not even the police."

The man sat in Makaroff's chair and lit a cigarette, Wozzeck could see the epitome of Englishness in him, he was polite to a fault, he offered Wozzeck a Silk Cut and half a bottle of Bell's, in two minutes he would pat Jerzy on the back and then push him into the river, "There is no escape," the man was saying. "Once you work for UniRex you are employed forever, or at least until we have decided to terminate the relationship. We do not look kindly upon those who turn their backs on us. You know the business we are in and so like all those who possess knowledge you possess also a powerful weapon to turn against us."

"My lips are sealed, I swear it, I have forgotten what UniRex is, I do not even remember Rita, who is Rita? Don't ask, I cannot tell you."

"Ah, yes. Dear Rita. Still in Paris, you know, our Rita. An excellent worker, Rita, one could almost say she was one of the boys. You see? With one word you could destroy your former lover as well as those men who paid you handsomely for your services. That is no way to treat your benefactors, now is it, Wozzeck?"

"But I am forever grateful, I will sign a statement to this effect, oh man, am I fucked but good."

The man smiled, one can smile and smile and be a villain, *Hamlet* was such a hit whenever it was played in Poland, there is no need to ask why.

"Come," said the man as he rose from his chair, "I want to show you something."

He led Wozzeck out to his car, a silver Rolls-Royce parked on Brewer Street, a shining temptation in the heart of sleaze, and of course Wozzeck made a strong protest, he was due to play his piano at the Blue Pussycat Club, one could not copulate there without the sound of music, Makaroff insisted on it, Wozzeck said no.

"But you have no choice. You are no longer employed at the club," said the man as he started the engine, *vroom, whoosh.* "As a matter of fact, the club is no longer in existence. Oh, we'll reopen it sometime, make it into a profitable venture, a going concern and all that, but you know, dear boy, you owe your first allegiance to us."

They moved silently through the dirty streets, there were tourists, and people peddling vegetables and flesh and the devil, "My mother told me never to get into a car with a stranger," Wozzeck protested, but of course the man insisted he was not a stranger, he was a great friend, an ally, a mentor, my God, thought Wozzeck, he is right out of the play I saw the other night, the Pinter.

"Now you see that Chinese restaurant there," said the man in the gray suit. "That belongs to us, we bought it out three years ago. I recommend it highly."

"Yes, I shall remember that, I shall take my wife and mother-in-law there, they are enamored of Chinese food, we shall go nowhere else. Now I must say goodbye to you here and now."

The man parked the car in front of the restaurant, people fled in terror when they saw it. A Chinese man in a black suit stepped out and pressed his hands together as if he were praying for his life, "Come here, Fung," the man in the gray suit and shades said, and of course Fung had no choice, he was beside himself with joy, he had heard his master's voice. "Fung, I want you to meet Wozzeck, say How d'ye do, Fung old boy. Tell me, Fung, how's business been lately?"

"Ah, excellent, excellent."

"Ah, good. I was just showing my good friend Wozzeck the sights. This is Greek Street, am I right, Fung?"

"Yes, sir, Greek Street," Wozzeck could not catch the drift the conversation was taking.

"And you are the finest restaurateur on Greek Street, am I right, Fung old chap?"

Clearly Fung had been through this form of interrogation before, he was sweating, sweating and remembering when it had all begun, he could also see his own funeral pass by him, papier mâché lions and firecrackers and clouds of incense, Wozzeck suspected it would be a beautiful sight to gladden the hearts of Fung's ancestors, he would bet that Fung could use Charlie Chan on the double.

"Have you got anything for me today, Fung old bean?"

"Ah, no, sir."

"Nothing? This is indeed a surprise."

Wozzeck was lost in the funhouse, he could not understand a word they were saying, and yet he remembered once in Paris watching the film *Kiss of Death* on television, suddenly the subtitles disappeared, but he could see how things were going, it was going to be blood in the gutter all the way to the end, one did not have to understand English to catch the meaning of Richard Widmark's laughter. And now things were not looking very good for him either, especially when the man in the gray suit unleashed his stiletto and tickled the throat of Fung. "Things had better improve by midnight, you understand, my good man?"

And Fung was grateful, grateful and in terror for his life, as the silver Rolls-Royce left him far behind, standing on the pavement and trembling.

"You like jazz, don't you, Wozzeck?"

"Yes, yes, you might say that, I—"

The man slid a cassette into his player and pressed a switch. A big band played "Strangers in the Night," it was not jazz, not at all, but who was Wozzeck to argue, he snapped his fingers and nodded his head and wondered when he was going to die. They stopped at a cinema on Windmill Street, one that was not showing a Jerry Lewis festival, it was clearly no place for Heidi, but rather a couple of flicks featuring the undraped female form and lengths of chain and people like Gino, who were well-hung and had nothing better to do with themselves. And no sooner had they parked in front of it than a man stepped out, all smiles in a cheap suit, and greeted the man in gray as if he were his long-lost brother, he even threw money at him, the man in the shades, and invited him and Wozzeck to view his latest epic, *Sex The rapist* the sign outside said, until the man explained that some joker had been fucking around with the letters, it was really called *Sex Therapist*, a great hit with the medical establishment.

But the man in the gray suit and dark glasses explained that he had to move on, he had much to show his friend Wozzeck, who was not in a gray suit but wearing rather a leather jacket and jeans and a flat-cap and looked so out of place in the Rolls that he hoped policemen all over London would spot the anomaly and save his life, fast.

They drove down Oxford Street, and here too the man in gray pointed out places that were owned by UniRex, shops selling blue jeans and stolen radios and video recorders. They went to Chelsea and cruised down the King's Road, there were bizarre young people there, they were everywhere, Wozzeck wondered what satanic organization these people with pink hair and razor blades belonged to, little did he suspect these were Maggie's unemployed minions. The man indicated expensive clothing shops called Blast and Flash and Piss Off, which were owned by UniRex, and also newsstands and the like, and although Wozzeck was certain that the finale of this little tour would be his own demise, he was shocked and surprised to find himself dropped off at his house off Archway Road, "We'll speak to you soon," the man said, and then he was gone. It was later that night that Wozzeck became aware of the fact that something within him had been destroyed, and he wondered how long ago the seed of destruction had been planted.

* * *

It was the speed, he knew that, of course he did, as he lay beside Heidi and listened to his Walkman, Miles Davis blowing his head off in a Chicago nightclub. If UniRex didn't get him first the drug would. He began to note the symptoms, he could feel the mind-numbing itch under his skin, he could feel his loose teeth and the way his hair seemed to have turned to hay, it was dry as tinder, he could become a living torch. And though he was killing off brain cells at the rate of ten thousand a day, he could see things with a certain lucidity, he could trace the course of his slow death, and he suspected that were it just the speed he might survive it, one could put up with the itch and the fear of the old pain, the old misery. No, no, that alone was not killing him, it was life itself that was doing it, that old cliché, a life of slavery, of fear, he was forever on the run, the bodies had already piled up in France and there were more to come, it was a life devoid of rules, of morals, of charity and second thoughts, a life of spontaneous violence, a gunshot in the night, a pool of blood, a knife slashing a throat, and no regrets, "We are returning to Paris," Kupki was saying, and suddenly it was morning.

* * *

"So you are abandoning your best friends," Wozzeck said as he helped Heidi's mama cook breakfast. "This is a very pretty thing, Kupki, I expected better from you, one does not leave a friend in need. Mama, there is shell in this egg, you are not being careful, soon you will be emptying the rubbish into our breakfast, cigarette butts and old shoes, be careful, old woman, there is a law against poisoning your devoted son-in-law."

"It is my idea," said Ludmilla. "I miss Paris."

"You miss Paris? I miss Paris too, what I don't miss is being hunted down day in day out by men in gray suits," and of course he remembered that the men in the gray suits were in London as well, it was a mad world.

"I dreamed about a man in a gray suit last night," said Mama as she dropped another eggshell into the frying pan.

"I am not surprised," said Wozzeck, who was unusually short on words that morning, due to the fact that eight minutes earlier, when he was getting out of his bath, he had glanced out the window and had seen the silver Rolls-Royce parked across the road from the house.

Even Heidi had noticed the change in him, he was no longer his old devil-may-care self, drumming out intricate solos on the furniture, whistling note-for-note Charlie Parker flights of fancy, he had become moody, withdrawn, he scratched his body and shut his eyes, and once she even caught him whispering to his reflection in the mirror, it was a frightening display, Jack Nicholson would have been proud of her husband.

"I wish to go to the British Museum," she had said earlier, and of course Wozzeck would not be able to join her, it was certain death should he take one step out of the apartment. "An excellent idea, my duckling," he said, "go to the British Museum and look at the statues and have a good time, I shall stay here and think about things."

But that was exactly what she didn't want him to do, thinking had such a detrimental effect on him, look at what it did to that girl in *The French Lieutenant's Woman*, so pretty and such a nervous wreck, sometimes Heidi wished that Jeremy Irons had simply pushed her into the sea and gone back to his fiancée, it was not worth the trouble hanging around a seaside village.

They sat down and began to eat their communal breakfast, Wozzeck throwing savage looks at Mama as he picked alien substances out of his egg, it was odd that no one else complained of it. "So you are going back to Paris, you and Ludmilla. So. Very nice. Yes, I wish you well, I hope you have enjoyed your stay here in London at my expense, now you can go back and tell Fetler and Bindler and Blotnik all about Jerzy and Heidi and Mama Dustbin there, tell them how nice we have been to you, how graciously we have treated our best friends."

"I am most grateful for your hospitality," said Kupki.

"Oh, me too," said Ludmilla of the plump breast and seductive eye.

"And of course you fully realize that once you get back to Paris you will walk right back into those men's hands, there is no way out, and what a pity it will be when we miss your funeral, I do so enjoy a good party."

And so they went, Ludmilla and Andrzej, and even Wozzeck wept as they left, he knew he would never see his friends again, it was the second worst moment of his life, the worst being when that bastard Kupki had said "Listen," he would never forgive him, not for a million years. "Goodbye," he said, "Goodbye my dear friends," and "Goodbye," he said to Heidi and her mama as they went off for a day's outing among the tombs and funeral offerings of the British Museum, he hoped they'd come up with a good design for his own forthcoming demise.

The silver Rolls had disappeared, and Wozzeck debated whether to leave the apartment, the man might be waiting for him, he might have parked around the corner, he might even be sitting out of Wozzeck's vision in his car, idling the engine and planning on running him down the moment he placed a foot on Archway Road. But there was no need for him to fear that, since fifteen minutes after Heidi and Mama had left for the museum there was a knock at the door, Wozzeck thought it might be his landlord, and what a surprise it was to see the man in the gray suit, there was mischief afoot.

"So, Wozzeck, we meet again. Lovely day, isn't it?"

And Wozzeck was puzzled, because it was raining cats and dogs, it was not lovely, not even passably nice, and he thought this must be some strange quirk in the English character, this spartan acceptance of misery as something no less exciting than the reissue of a long-lost recording by the legendary Bud Powell.

"Today," the man went on as he took a seat, made himself at home, picked idly at the magnificent fabric that covered the sofa and successfully masqueraded as a rag, "today I have some news for you. Word has reached me of a certain little task we wish you to perform. It will not take too much of your time, and you might even find it enjoyable."

"No, my time is valuable, I am afraid I can do nothing more for you, let us shake hands and part as friends," and Wozzeck sat on the sofa and rested his face in his hands, the power of "No" was no longer worth a sou.

"I am afraid you haven't a choice, Wozzeck. You see, you owe us some more of your time. Your work in Paris was never successfully completed. Think of it this way, Jerzy. If, say, you were working for our friends in America you would be treated more harshly. They would not give you a second chance. They are ruthless men, our American cousins, they do not take at all kindly to disloyalty, they practice the kiss of death. But here in Britain, you see, we go about things differently, we have a high regard for human life, we enjoy the freedom of choice."

Wozzeck looked up at the man in the gray suit and shades, at the smile and the cigarette and the furled umbrella that picked out circles on the linoleum, and he knew that the words he had just heard were simply that, words, sounds without significance worth no more than a "Good morning" or "Sorry" or "How are you, mate," he'd just as soon stab Wozzeck in the back.

"I'm afraid, however, that your choice is now limited to saying 'Yes.'"

"A task," said Wozzeck, "and what happens afterward, are there more tasks and do I have to make up for my other sins, yes, this is true?"

"No," the man said gently, "once you have completed this little job for us you will be free," and this word was like music to Jerzy's ears, it was a solo by Mingus, plucked strings and shouts of joy, twelve bars by Miles, muted and seductive, even a single note by Monk, eccentric and resonant of liberation, so this was the end, well and truly the finale of his tale.

"I need guarantees," said Wozzeck, and then shut his mouth, he did not want to spoil the moment, he had made such a bloody mess of his life so far.

"You're learning fast," the man in the gray suit said as he rose and looked around the sitting room, perhaps the most depressing sitting room in all of Britain, everything was brown and screamed of 1946. "Yes, I will give you guarantees."

"Nothing is to happen to Heidi, my wife, she is young and intelligent, she deserves to live."

"You have my word."

"And her mother, who is old and sometimes nasty, but who should be allowed to die in her bed when her time comes, I think she will thank me for that. And I am running low on speed, I need another few ounces, I cannot live without it."

"Ah," said the man, and that Ah was like a mystical incantation, the sound of a sphere, the Alpha and Omega of his slavery, "now you are touching upon a critical point. No, we do not wish to harm your wife or her mother. But we must be certain you will not run away this time, Wozzeck, your word is not enough."

"So you will not give me speed? No speed, no work, it is physically impossible for me to lift a finger without speed," and the man reached into his pocket and threw a small plastic envelope to Wozzeck, and the sight of the powder within it was enough to lift his spirits for at least twelve minutes, he thanked the man, he fell to his knees, he was a new man all over again.

"There will be a short period of training," the man in the gray suit said, placing the tip of his umbrella under Wozzeck's chin and lifting his face. "If at any time during this period you show even the slightest resistance the speed will be stopped and you will have to suffer the consequences. Furthermore, if you should make any attempt to flee Britain or contact the authorities we shall take reprisals against your family."

And suddenly there was an aura of fear about this scene, it was as if something had fled the space between them and the walls were closing in, Wozzeck could only think about the day he had heard martial law had been declared in his homeland, every future moment was a moment from the past, there was no escaping the dark age of Jerzy Wozzeck.

"There's this man, you see," the man was saying, Wozzeck had to keep his wits about him to follow his meaning, there was this man you see, the man in gray had said, a man, a man you see, "and, like you, he has not been loyal to us. But his disloyalty has gone much further than yours, Wozzeck, his case is very critical. He is an Englishman, about fifty years old. He is quite wealthy, he lives in Hampstead. Two years ago he owed some people a large sum of money. We helped him settle some of his debts and get back on his feet. But he has been ungrateful, this chap, and he has had some dealings with one of our competitors. We do not wish to say any more about this man, as we'd prefer you to learn about him for yourself. We should like you to make friends with him, to help him feel comfortable in your presence."

"Ah, that is not so bad, I am very good at making friends, it is one of my many gifts, I am amiable to a fault, I should be delighted to do this favor for you, I—"

"And then you will kill him, Wozzeck."

"Ah," and his "Ah" too was packed with meaning, it was an "Ah" of fear, the "Ah" that is heard when a man is about to fall off a cliff, drown in the Vistula, be tortured in a Warsaw prison cell. "Ahh," he cried.

# 7

LIFE WAS BECOMING A NIGHTMARE, NO EXAGGERATION, and he was confirmed in his judgment when later that day he took the tube to Leicester Square and strolled about as if in a daze, he could not fail to note that Fung's Chinese restaurant was shut due to a death in the family, it was an omen that spoke of his own brilliant future. He walked past Ronnie Scott's and even though Ronnie Scott did not wish to hire him just now or ever, even though Ronnie Scott was playing host to Art Blakey and the Jazz Messengers, even though Art Blakey had been around for what seemed like centuries, he did not feel the urge to return there that evening to see this man who must be at least two hundred and seventeen years old, he did not feel the urge because the urge for joy and emancipation had been replaced by an urge for an end to all his troubles, Job had nothing on him, not a single boil.

He walked past the nude revues and the people sitting in the entrances bade him enter in an English he was beginning to understand only too well, the English that says, "Come on, mate, there's fun inside," and "A fiver and you won't regret it," and there were smiles on the faces of all these people, smiles and skin eruptions. He walked over to Charing Cross Road and wandered through the bookshops and looked at the pretty new volumes all in a row, he wished he could read English, he wished he could better understand what in the British character was permitting these people to put him through so much torture. He went into a jazz record shop on Shaftsbury Avenue and flipped hungrily through the record albums, he counted twelve he would dearly have loved to buy had circumstances been otherwise, were he not condemned to murder a fellow human being and had he owned a turntable. So he bought a few cassettes, expensive American imports, what the hell, and he walked some more and listened to his music, he sat on a bench in Soho Square and listened to Art Tatum and wept and poked his fingers through the holes in his sneakers.

He hoped Heidi and Mama were enjoying themselves at the British Museum, he had always wanted to go there, the British Museum, but now he had lost the urge even to do that, such treasures in the midst of such tragedy. His grandpapa who had owned a delicatessen on Jerusalem Avenue would have understood him perfectly, he had lived through so much, Poland was Poland, all was well with the world, and then suddenly Poland was not Poland anymore, there was the sound of jackboots, screams in the night, the screech owl of history never sleeps.

Wozzeck descended underground.

A train was just pulling out, and there were nasty words from the others who had just missed it, because they were condemned to stand in the airless heat for what could be hours, nothing was dependable anymore, not in London. He examined the tube map and mopped his brow and switched on Art Tatum and watched the little scoreboard that told you through the marvels of electronics which train was coming and when it was due to arrive. There were rats and mice, furry beasts of uncertain temperament, racing between the tracks, hunting down weaker creatures, squealing with delight among the discarded cigarette packs, and Wozzeck wondered if they had gone blind from living in eternal semidarkness, and speculated on where the bats hung out, and why everything down in the bowels of London smelled like World War II, it was ungodly in more ways than one.

He knew his train was the one that terminated at High Barnet, he watched the score and saw that his was first and the one behind it, the one going to Golders Green, was second, it was six minutes against twelve, it was a race to the finish. Now his train was due in four minutes, four minutes until relief, four minutes, and now three, he took off his earphones and listened expectantly for the sound of the wheels, *clicketyclack*, and the screech of brakes, and he knew the man in the gray suit and shades was watching him from the other end of the platform, London was a prison, they had been onto him from the year one. And now it was one minute until the train was due, one minute, the screen was about to change, there was the sound of the modern age fluttering within the mechanism, and then suddenly he saw that his train had disappeared, only the one going to Golders Green was due to arrive, and he wondered what had happened to the train, if someone had stolen it, or if it had gotten caught in a time warp, the passengers were in for a big shock, a close encounter they would regret for eternity. And so he took the other train, the wrong one, to Camden Town and crossed the platform to get onto the correct one, the heat was unbelievable, he thought his skin would burst, he felt like a sausage, and as he boarded the next train for Archway and descended for the short walk home he thought again of the terrifying scene in the Underground in *The Devil Wears a Figleaf*, and wondered why life was imitating art, why couldn't it have been *The Night Before Christmas* or *Gone With the Wind*, something he could rely on to get him through this bloody awful mess.

Heidi still had not come home, he hoped she was enjoying her travels through the British Museum, finally he was alone, there was peace, brief as it would turn out to be. He snorted some more speed and ate a strawberry trifle and drank some tea, it was a hundred and seven outside and still rising, and afterward he listened to Radio 3 on his Walkman, something ominous by Schnittke, it no longer mattered.

And as he wandered aimlessly through the apartment he began to realize that there was something different about it, someone had been there during his absence and had left his calling card, drawers were not shut, everything had been searched, and that didn't matter either, UniRex had their hands on all areas of his life, even his underpants in the top drawer.

The man knocked at the door just after three, while Wozzeck was napping, he had switched to a play on Radio 4, about a housewife who goes insane and runs rampant with her iron, and had fallen into a deep dreamless sleep, even though the housewife stayed awake and was left helping the police with their inquiries, i.e., in jail.

"You had a good day, I hope?" said the man as he pointed out the window with his umbrella. "At least the rain has stopped. It's hot, though, isn't it. They say it will rain again."

Wozzeck did not know how to respond, to talk of the weather at such a time seemed irrelevant and perhaps even sacrilegious.

"We understand your friend Kupki and his lovely wife left for Paris this morning. I'm afraid to say that they didn't get very far. Something unavoidable came up to delay their return."

And of course Wozzeck knew what it was that had delayed them, it was the men in gray suits and dark glasses, "You are insane," he told the man, and all the man could do was laugh.

"You see, Jerzy, had it been you who had decided to leave Britain all we would have had to do was contact both Lunel's boys and the Sûreté and finger you as the chap who did in the late Rocco. The evidence is all in place, you see, you wouldn't have stood a chance. Lunel's lieutenants would have gotten to you even before you could ring up a solicitor."

"So what is it, you have killed Kupki and Ludmilla, they are harmless people, they wouldn't have hurt a flea."

"But Kupki knows too much, you see, there are innocent lives at stake here, Wozzeck, you must see it from our point of view."

Wozzeck began to grow worried as to the fate of Heidi and Mama, it was late, they should have been home already, there is so much to see at the British Museum, for them there is always tomorrow and the next day.

"And don't worry about your wife and the old girl," the man reassured him. "I'm certain they're perfectly safe, they'll be home soon."

"What, you have taken them, kidnapping is a crime," he knew it was a lost cause, these men did not know remorse from a bowl of pea soup, they couldn't care less.

The man in gray handed Wozzeck a photograph, a man waiting for a taxi. "This is the chap you're going to kill, Wozzeck."

"Yes, fine, this is the man I am going to kill, what, I am going to bite him to death?"

"Tonight I shall pick you up promptly at nine. At that time you will be taken to a warehouse outside London. There you will begin your training in the use of firearms. We shall provide the weapon, and you, dear boy, will provide the manpower." And the man left him with two hundred pounds toward his rent and yet another ounce of speed, it was like Christmas in August, save that Santa was Satan, Wozzeck mused over this little word game, he thought he might be on to something.

Now Wozzeck knew very well he was incapable of killing his fellow man. He stood by the window and looked upon gray Highgate and wondered if the impulse that was now rising in him should be encouraged, if he should go to the police and blow UniRex sky-high, the temptation was almost more than he could bear.

An hour later he was standing in Highgate police station and trying to make himself understood, trying very hard to recall phrases from his language tape, it was ridiculous.

"Look," he said finally in Polish, "I have come to report a crime that will take place very soon, there are these men, these men in gray suits and shades, UniRex, dig? And these guys are everywhere, they are murderers and drug traffickers."

Of course the police could not understand a word he was saying, it was all Greek to them, he tried it in French and German and even Russian, and all they could speak was English, the world was a closed book to them. And when he finally left the station unsatisfied, cap in hand, he saw the silver Rolls parked across the road, and in the reflection of the sunset he could see too that the Rolls was just like the man who drove it: inscrutable, with darkened windows.

Heidi and Mama had arrived a few minutes before he returned to the apartment. They had had a splendid time. Good. They had eaten cheesecake and drunk tea in the museum cafeteria. Good. They had bought souvenirs and postcards to send to Kupki and Ludmilla, there was a funny one that reminded Heidi of her Leipzig friend Hannah's mama, a chess queen with her hand to her face apparently saying *oy vey*. "Good," said Wozzeck, he could not get a word in edgewise.

"And Mama and I have had a long talk," she went on, "we have decided to return to Paris."

"Bad," said Wozzeck. "This is not possible, you cannot make even the slightest effort to do so, otherwise you will be in for big trouble, please do not ask me to elaborate."

Of course Mama was enjoying herself immensely, watching him squirm and unable to put in his two *zlotys*. Finally he managed to get Heidi into the bedroom, he sat her on the bed and spoke quietly, like the reasonable man he was, as if he were trying to sell her an insurance policy, he had seen it once in a film, "I have to make a confession," he began.

He told her about the men in gray suits and dark glasses and about his addiction, he spoke too of the murder he was being asked to commit, and he promised her that after he had put this man in the grave he would be able to go to Paris with her, the heat would be off and all that remained would be a one-way trip to hell for little Jerzy Wozzeck. And of course Heidi wept and screamed and threw her British Museum postcards at him, even the queen saying *oy vey*, he was a dirty fucker, she said, a dirty fucker and a stupid, yes, he was a stupid, she repeated, and he could not but agree with her, he was a dirty fucker and a stupid, "and don't forget shithead," he said, "I am most certainly the shithead of the month."

"And stupid!"

"Yes, yes, an excellent point, it is worthwhile reiterating it, I have been stupid and at this very moment am suffering pangs of total idiocy, but like it or not, *meine Liebe*, unless you want this stupid to end up sleeping with the fishes he will have to kill a strange man, aged fifty, now living in Hampstead."

Finally she calmed down, and after her tears had dried she sat on the bed and stared at him as if he were only a vaguely familiar stranger, it was eerie and unsettling for him, but there it was, she stared at him as if he were Honoré de Balzac come back from the last dead century, I have seen that face before, she is thinking.

"So, *voilà*, there it is," he said. "I am sorry, I am doubly sorry, you did not deserve any of this, but now I will try to get you out of it."

"So," she said, and all he wanted was a word from her, a phrase, even a punch in the face would have satisfied him, anything.

"I hate London," she said.

"You are perhaps being a little harsh. You have just spent the whole bloody day gazing at the glories of the British Museum, no one hurt you, yes? No one made illicit and unseemly advances, no? So do not complain, London may be perfectly nice, I would be the first to agree if I did not have to murder one of its residents."

"So what are you going to do?" she asked as she changed her clothes, they were drenched in perspiration.

"I am going to murder one of its residents, what do you think I am going to do."

"And what am I supposed to do with Mama during all of this?"

"I shall murder her too, it will be one less mouth to feed."

"I hate you, Jerzy, you can go to hell, you bastard."

"I was only joking, when I go to hell I shall be the resident comedian, I and twenty million other jokers."

"So what happens now?" she asked.

"Tonight they are going to take me to some warehouse it is, I think, and there they will teach me how to kill a resident of London, aged fifty, very rich."

"And what if you don't come back?"

"Then you will know for sure, my little dumpling, that a Polish resident of Paris, temporarily in London, aged thirty-eight and impoverished, was killed instead."

Heidi considered this for a moment, "And what happens afterward, after you kill this man?"

"Then we can go home and forget that I killed a man, even though my conscience will keep me awake for the remainder of my short life."

"He promised you it would be all over?"

"Yes, my darling Leipziger, afterward we can all wake up from this nightmare and go home to Paris. Then I can try to find another job with some other gangster, and we shall end up back where we started, sitting in London and waiting for me to kill a man."

He decided against telling Heidi about Kupki and Ludmilla, for it was not yet entirely clear to him what had happened to his two friends, he did not know that at that very moment they were not terribly happy with the man known as Jerzy Wozzeck.

Heidi buttoned her blouse and tucked it into her jeans and gazed here and there, it was an old family sign that she was thinking matters over, sometimes she reminded him of a little bird, he wanted to eat her up. "So you kill this man," she said. "So what? He is nobody we know, what does it matter?"

And suddenly he did not want to eat her up, she was missing the point altogether, "It matters, believe me, number one because I have no desire to kill a fellow human being, and number two because when I am the man pulling the trigger, it matters, believe me, it matters."

They ate dinner in silence, at least Heidi and Wozzeck did, for something had loosened Mama's tongue, she was like the voice that tells you the time over and over again on the telephone, it does not shut up until you hang the damn thing on the hook. "Mama," Wozzeck said gently, and "Excuse me," and so forth, and still she went on, about the war, her husband, about Uncle Hermann and how he once put a lit pipe in his pocket and oh boy was he in for a big surprise, and about how her old friend Elisabeth once bit into some strudel and broke her front teeth and about the time Mama had taken a taxi to Wolfgang Rathauser's house and Wolfgang was drunk and almost ninety and still trying to take liberties with her, and also about how once Furtwängler had a bit too much to drink and danced a jig and nearly killed the cat, and eventually even Heidi was growing disenchanted with these endless tales of the old country and so she demanded silence and of course Mama burst into tears, "You never loved me," she cried, "you never loved me, I am an old woman, let me die in peace," etc., and of course Wozzeck had to leave the table, it was a quarter to nine, and when he went into the bedroom to get his jacket and cap he buried his face in the pillow and screamed obscenities in four different languages, and afterward as he waited outside for the silver Rolls he contemplated offering Heidi's mama to the sinister and deadly men in gray, she would talk them to death.

* * *

The warehouse, Wozzeck estimated, was an hour's drive from Highgate. Or perhaps it was more like half an hour, maybe even fifteen minutes, it is impossible to tell when you are riding in a car with darkened windows and the voice of Frank Sinatra blasting at you from eight speakers, "Strangers in the Night" and all that implies.

There were three other men in the car, one driving, of course, and one beside him, operating the volume control, and a man in a gray suit and shades sitting beside Wozzeck, it was his old friend with the umbrella, soon, thought Jerzy, he will stick the thing up my backside and shoot a deadly pellet into my bloodstream, it was how they went about things here in London.

"Wozzeck," the man said gently in his elegant French, "Wozzeck, I saw you today. I saw you go into the police station. So you decided to do the one honest thing, did you?"

"No, no, you have got it all wrong, I was merely asking directions, Highgate is an enigma to me."

"You were telling them about us, Wozzeck, I am certain of it. Let me remind you that were you even able to speak English the authorities would not take notice of what you have to say about UniRex. Do you know why this is so? It is because the authorities are unaware of us, established as we are. You see, we are a large international corporation, we extend our influence into all areas of life, but we operate beneath the surface, we are like an underground spring that refreshes those who are not even aware of the source."

"We're even fully computerized," said the passenger in the front seat, the one in control of the entertainment. He ejected the Sinatra tape and put in something else and then pressed the appropriate button, Wozzeck could not quite follow the procedure, and then of course it was Maria the Greek singing "Divinités du Styx" and Wozzeck suspected this trip would not include a return journey, "Oh man," he said, resting his head against the window.

"In any event," the man with the umbrella said, "the very fact that you did go to the police means that you have forfeited one of your guarantees. If you do not carry out your orders I will be forced to take your wife."

It took Wozzeck a few minutes to accustom himself to the shadows and dimness of the warehouse, and when he could finally take it all in he saw that it contained many things of interest, old cars, disassembled motors, sealed aluminum containers, even a selection of shop-window dummies, it was impossible to say exactly what the place was used for. The man with the umbrella led Wozzeck to a locked office, and inside of course was a wide array of firearms and such, the man was proud of his collection, it was like Al Capone's playroom, Death City.

"The entire structure is fully soundproofed. One could fire three hundred rounds from this Soviet machine gun and no one, not even someone standing outside by the car, would be able to hear it."

"That is reassuring," said Wozzeck, and he supposed too that no one would be able to hear the high-pitched sounds of someone being tortured, he did not like the way things were going, not one bit. The man took a pistol from the table and showed it to Wozzeck. "This is the weapon you'll be using. It's custom-made, quite lightweight—go on, hold it in your hand—naturally it carries no serial number and yet even though it looks quite like a toy it can blow a man apart. Silently. Especially if you use the right kind of cartridge." He held up the bullet and displayed it in front of Wozzeck's eyes. "This too is custom-made. Once it makes impact it explodes into a thousand fragments. A very effective piece of ammunition."

"Yes, yes, this is all very nice, all I wish to know is why you cannot murder this man yourself, why count on an amateur like myself, I will point the thing and pull the trigger and find only that I have removed one of my own toes in addition to half the floor."

"We cannot do the job ourselves because we are known to this man. And we don't go in for bombs or sniper killings. All we want is a nice quiet intimate murder. Oh yes, we could pay a professional to do this job for us, money is no object. But as you owe us a favor we thought we might put you to use. Think about it, Wozzeck, think how splendid it will be acting like a responsible citizen and coming to the aid of your fellow man."

"And what happens afterward, after I blow this man apart, what happens to me then?"

"But I've already told you, Wozzeck, you will be perfectly free."

"Yes, yes, I am aware of that, but not two minutes ago in the car you told me that the authorities would never believe me if I told them about you, so I am no risk to your corporation, I beg of you to let me go."

"Of course that's true. But it isn't the authorities we're concerned about, it's the competition. UniRex is only one of many large organizations. If anyone spoke to a member of the competition about us we would be in grave danger. That is why we must secure your silence."

And Wozzeck knew that just as in Paris he would be tied to this crime, his signature would be left everywhere, even his image, Wozzeck with gun in hand, would be indelibly impressed upon his victim's pupils for the whole world to gaze at in wonder.

"If you do your job well, Wozzeck, you can return to Paris as if nothing at all had happened."

"That is most amusing, I return to France and then they arrest me for killing Rocco Lunel."

The man smiled and took the gun from Wozzeck's hand. "Not if we can provide a suitable suspect. And altering the evidence is no problem, we have friends in the Sûreté. Of course you may still have to answer for the death of our friend on the train."

"Ah, but my mother-in-law was responsible for that one, let me refer her to you, she summers in Berchtesgaden."

"Just fulfill your obligation, Wozzeck, and let us take care of the rest. Do your job efficiently and we will support your habit. We may even be willing to turn a blind eye to the little incident on the train. Be efficient, Wozzeck, and we will make sure your friend and his wife survive the end of August."

"Kupki and Ludmilla, what, you have them, they are well, I do not understand."

"Oh yes, they are well. At the moment they're staying at a farmhouse in Brittany. They're being fed and are living in more comfort than I daresay they're accustomed to. But they know what you must do, and they also know that their future depends on your ability to carry out this little mission. Otherwise, you see, things could get complicated. Now before we instruct you on how to use this firearm I should like you to know some more facts about your victim."

One of the other men in gray took the covers off a television set and a video recorder and pressed various buttons and turned knobs. Immediately a film of the front of a house began: a door opened, a man in a dark suit descended the steps and walked away.

"His name is Ian Graham. Currently he deals in antiques and is quite well-respected by his colleagues in the trade. He's part-owner of a shop located on Bond Street. He is an educated man. He was two years ahead of me at Trinity. Ah. I can see this means nothing to you."

"Nothing, nothing at all, I find even the Underground confusing—"

"Which is precisely what we hoped would be the case. You wouldn't, then, feel uneasy around him because of the obvious discrepancy between your respective social classes."

"Yes, fine, but this man wears a tie, he is rich, he would not want to be seen dead with someone like me around, no, no, I have got that wrong, he would not want to be seen alive with me, dead is the whole idea, I dig, be cool."

"Let me assure you that Mr. Graham will have no qualms about your presence. He speaks fluent French. He has a deep and abiding love of music. You will have much to talk about." And what he failed to add, the man with the umbrella, was that they had let it be known to Ian Graham that he was already a marked man, that his murderer could turn up at any time, the men in gray have a profound adoration of sport and a highly developed sense of fair play.

"Two days a week," the man continued, the screen was showing the front of an antiques shop, people were not exactly kicking down the door, undoubtedly this was not a place where you could pick up a piece of useless junk for a few *zlotys*, "Tuesdays and Thursdays, Graham works at his shop. On the other days he remains at home, sometimes leaving for a lunch appointment or dinner. Occasionally he attends a concert or the opera. In fact, I would say that right now he is at the Albert Hall, listening to the Promenade Concert—what's on tonight?" he asked one of his cronies in gray.

"*The Damnation of Faust*, Elder conducting."

"He is perhaps even following along with a pocket score. Now let us go and make some music of our own."

They left the office, the man locked it, they went into the central portion of the warehouse. One of the other men had set up a target, a plaster life-sized man sitting in a chair, it was uncanny, they had dressed the dummy and painted in facial features, and he was smiling at Wozzeck, he was saying "Please kill me, Jerzy, there's a good chap."

The man with the umbrella marked a spot on the floor about eight paces from the mannequin. "The old boy's got a small living room," he kindly informed Wozzeck. "Now put the pistol in your pocket. No, your jacket pocket, it has a hair-spring trigger, you will blow your balls to smithereens if you sit the wrong way." Wozzeck did as he was told, he felt like John Wayne and he preferred not to feel like John Wayne, he preferred real men like Thelonious Monk and Cab Calloway. "Now, let us pretend you are having a little chat with Graham, shall we? Let's say you are discussing music. You are speaking about the influence of jazz on Igor Stravinsky," and suddenly Wozzeck had nothing to say on the subject, the circumstances were not quite right, music and violence did not mix, it was like a combination of borscht and floor polish, it was best to keep away from so lethal a cocktail.

"And now, very calmly, remove the pistol, aim it at the man's face and fire."

Of course the pistol got caught on the edge of his pocket and naturally he was not very calm at all, for he had the bright idea to turn the thing on the men in gray suits, he could have sent them all to an early grave, and it was an idea that occupied him for at least thirty seconds, until he saw that one of the other men had a machine gun in his hands and was having no compunctions about turning it on Wozzeck, he counted for nothing in this world, not a piano-playing Pole.

"Now try it again, Wozzeck. Take it calmly and smoothly out of your pocket, yes, that's it, aim it steadily at the man's head, no, you don't need to use both hands, you have been watching too many American films, that's it, it's quite light, now just squeeze the trigger," and before he knew what had happened there was a dull thud and the dummy was minus one part of his body, namely his torso, and Jerzy watched bemusedly and with growing horror a plaster head rolling toward him, smiling all the way and no longer much interested in Stravinsky and jazz.

"Next time aim a bit higher," the man with the umbrella said.

# 8

YOU REMEMBER THAT FILM WITH THE ACTOR YOU LIKE, the blonde?"

Heidi thought for a moment, put her finger at the corner of her mouth, set down her book, "Robert Redford?" she said.

"No, no, the other one, he is English, thin as a rail, the one who must shoot de Gaulle."

"*The Day of the Jackal*," she said, "Edward Fox, 1973," she was a walking encyclopedia of film.

"Yes, you have hit the jackpot, and guess what, I am to play in the remake of *The Day of the Jackal*, except my target will not be so conspicuous. Here is my gun," he said, brandishing the object and laying it carefully down on the table, even if you breathed on it it could go off and blow your beloved to kingdom come, "here is the ammunition, and here is Jerzy Wozzeck. Our victim at this very moment lies in bed in Hampstead, dreaming of paradise, little does he know that I am being forced to empty his cranial cavity some day soon."

They had kept him at the warehouse until he could shoot a man between the eyes without even thinking about it, it was half-past two, Heidi's mama was fast asleep, Jerzy was in a sweat. He told Heidi what the man in the gray suit had informed him, that his victim would be happy to have him for a friend, that soon after they had become inseparable he was to shoot the man between the eyes, and after that he was to dial a certain telephone number, "and once they have seen the dirty work for themselves, once they have examined the brain tissue splattered on the walls and concluded it belongs to the man with the hole in his head, they will let us go back to Paris, Mama and all."

"You are certain, you are sure they aren't lying?"

"I have a choice what to believe?"

He slipped into bed beside Heidi, he was so distressed that he had forgotten to take off his sneakers.

"Maybe we can just leave, they will never know what happened to us."

"Yes, that is brilliant, Heidi, magnificent, you think I don't come up with ideas like that myself? It would be an excellent idea except that UniRex has people everywhere, in New York, Alaska, the South Pole, the West is run by these gangsters, they probably even handle the catering for the White House. Besides, if I don't do the job they will kill Kupki and Ludmilla. Kupki I might not miss so much, he got me into this thing, but Ludmilla is a different matter, oh man is she ever, she is a masterpiece of human nature and beauty. Now I am hungry, I am going to cook an egg."

They went over the details for the hundredth time, they watched the sunrise and then the clouds roll in and the inevitable rain fall on the grateful people of London, Wozzeck ate five eggs and drank six glasses of tea and looked around the room and was miserable. "It would not be so bad if they asked me to rob someone or to give some guy a little push in a dark alley. But to ask me to kill someone, me, a sensitive person with a possibly brilliant future and who is also, incidentally, a coward, is going too far."

Heidi did not know whether to soothe her husband and reassure him that even as a murderer he would still be in her good graces or to recoil from him. She watched him sitting at the kitchen table in his underwear, scratching at his body and licking his lips and mumbling to himself, he was a pathetic sight, and then she had the further shock of observing him, for the first time in her innocent life, take his dose of speed, it was a bizarre ritual, the dividing of the powder, and the funny way it disappeared up his nose—zipp!—and it was gone.

After a few glorious moments he was back to his old self, the man she had married all those years ago in Warsaw in his ill-fitting brown suit, except he was a different man now, he was a junkie and a murderer-to-be, Clint Eastwood had nothing on him because Clint Eastwood and not Jerzy Wozzeck looked like he would blow your brains out for two francs, you would run like hell. "So what are you going to do?" she asked.

"I am going to kill this Ian Graham, otherwise my brilliant future goes right down the drain like a rotten head of cabbage. Ah, here is Mama, *guten Morgen*, Mama, you slept well, yes? We kept you awake, perhaps? Isn't it a glorious day? How about a nice long walk in the rain, say six hundred miles up to Scotland, eh?"

"Oh, stop it, Jerzy," said Heidi as she went to prepare breakfast for her mother.

Wozzeck switched on the radio and pulled on his trousers, the news as far as he could understand it was not good, the President of the United States, star of stage, screen, and radar, had sometime earlier prayed for the souls of SS men, and now everyone had forgotten it, he was as beloved as ever, all was forgiven, and Wozzeck could think only of *Nineteen Eighty-Four*, where it was bliss to believe that two and two made five, except that it was now 1985, nobody was aware it was still *Nineteen Eight-Four* and that it would be *Nineteen Eighty-Four* even in 1986 and 1987 and 2001, it had been *Nineteen Eighty-Four* since 1914 and still nobody realized it, Big Brother lives forever in the minds of the unthinking billions. Even the weather told this tale, there was a huge depression over Britain, it would be there for the foreseeable future, and what the weatherman failed to mention was that it had been there since the year 0, since the days of King Canute and Nat King Cole and Henry IV Part One, and would probably be there forever, beyond the foreseeable future, at least until the end of *Nineteen Eighty-Four*, which for Jerzy might come, the way things were now looking, sometime before the end of the week.

"I am going out," he said to Heidi, and of course she asked him where he could possibly go, and although he agreed with her, to go anywhere, to do anything, would seem irrelevant in the circumstances, he took his leather jacket and flat-cap and went out anyway, it was better than sitting around and listening to Mama trying to put her East German teeth back into her mouth.

He took the Underground to Camden Town, he knew the men in gray would be watching him, then changed for the tube to Hampstead. He strolled down Hampstead High Street, glanced at a jazz magazine at a newsstand, bought some Gitanes and matches, smoked a cigarette, turned onto Gayton Road, where the man he was going to murder lived. He was so nonchalant about it that people stared at him, the postman and the milkmen and even the blokes who were pretending to renovate houses and apartments, everyone looked at him because he smelled of death, he was the sick center of the world. He stood across the road from the house where the man lived and wondered which was his apartment, even though he had no intention of walking over and finding out. And for a moment, a split second, he had a genuinely empty feeling inside him, and for that split second he wished he had his gun with him, he could have walked across the road and done the man in without a second thought. He wondered if other people in the world understood this terrifying sensation, or if they didn't understand it did they at least experience it from time to time, and of course he had had his moment of enlightenment, he had seen into the black depths of humanity's soul and had glimpsed the great raw hollow; and he knew that should he fully succumb to it he would never be truly free, never, ever.

He walked down to the Heath and watched as a small dog pulled its master, an elderly bespectacled man with long white hair and a sullen disposition, and Wozzeck wondered if this man too had had this frightening vision, and he concluded that he had, for the man did not seem pleased with the ways of the world either.

The gypsies were in the Heath, they came running after him with shiny aluminum pails, small girls who demanded money from him, and of course he had no choice now, he threw fivers at them, he had seen into the soul of the world, the souls of those who have no need to beg for money, and yet who make beggars out of the rest of us.

He returned to the street where his victim lived, looking this way and that as if he were there for some purpose, perhaps to meet his stockbroker or investment counselor, and then suddenly he saw a man descend from the house, a man in a raincoat and soft leather shoes with little tassels, a man with a small cigar and plump cheeks, and Wozzeck knew this was his victim, he had caught the scent, he followed him to the High Street, followed him as he went into the supermarket and bought eggs and biscuits and a loaf of bread and streaky bacon, Wozzeck wanted to stop him, look him in the eye, and say, "Do not bother buying these, monsieur, for one day soon I am going to kill you," but he could not do so for he did not think he could kill this man, after all, this man or any other man, save perhaps Hitler, who conveniently was already dead.

For the next two days Wozzeck did not leave the apartment, he played cards with Heidi and her mama, he was no longer a citizen of 1984. He hoped the men in gray suits would forget about this little commission, and when he realized this would be an unlikely occurrence, akin to a cinema in Warsaw showing *Sex The rapist*, that their every thought was devoted to death and revenge, he changed his mind and hoped this Ian Graham might decide to kill himself, which would be a load off Wozzeck's mind, though he couldn't guarantee any rewards for the Englishman in his next life.

On the second day a large envelope was delivered to their apartment. Inside was a photograph of Kupki and Ludmilla looking as if they were saying, "Please, Wozzeck." Ludmilla was holding a copy of *Le Monde* of two days before, while Kupki was displaying a sign that in French requested that Wozzeck be quick about murdering this stranger who was nothing to him, for if he didn't his two friends who meant a great deal more to him would be tortured and killed and buried in unmarked graves in the Breton countryside.

"They are our best friends!" Heidi shrieked, she cried and cried until the landlord pounded on their door and asked if they were all right and said that he would very much appreciate it if they would pay him another month's rent for his four-room shithole, he was never quite himself, their landlord, it was best to placate the beast in man.

And so Wozzeck took the tube to Bond Street and walked up and down past Ian Graham's antiques shop and looked into other windows, at the expensive trinkets and overpriced vinyl handbags, and then he took the plunge and went into the antiques shop, the time had come to make his move. At once Ian Graham was by his side, clearly he did not trust the likes of Wozzeck to be left alone, as if he would attempt to run out into the street with a twelve-ton sideboard.

"Can I help you, sir?" and his "sir?" was so condescending that Wozzeck was quite certain Graham had said, "You are a shit, you little turd, and now if you will piss off out of here I will be eternally grateful, you might put off the other customers," even though there were no other customers, who could afford this junk, anyway?

"*Non, merci, monsieur*," said Wozzeck, he kept his hands behind his back and examined a painting of a horse.

"*Ah, je parle français, moi*," said Ian Graham, and at once, because he had been raised to respect all Continentals save the Wops and the dirty Spaniards and the Huns, he seemed to melt all over Wozzeck, he probably suspected he was a film director or a rock star, he was dressed like a slob, was Jerzy.

"*Ah, bon*," said Wozzeck. "I am only browsing."

"If you should need any assistance, sir … ?" and he kept a respectful distance, there was something familiar about this customer, Ian Graham was thinking, and he suspected he had seen his picture in *Harpers & Queen* or at last year's Academy Awards extravaganza, he congratulated himself on having recognized a Famous Person, he was in for a big shock.

When Wozzeck reached Archway tube station the silver Rolls-Royce was waiting for him. "You received the photograph, I hope?" the man with the umbrella asked. "Come, sit beside me, we have a matter to discuss." The driver put his foot down, and suddenly they were moving along at a healthy clip, Wozzeck guessed about a hundred and fifty miles an hour, and the man with the umbrella was asking Wozzeck what the delay was and why he hadn't completed his job.

"It's like this," said Wozzeck, and he explained that he hadn't found the opportunity to shoot Ian Graham, but he was working on it.

"You must go to his apartment, Wozzeck. Simply ring his bell and when he opens the door shoot him between the eyes, it's as simple as that."

"My mother-in-law has not been well, it has been most troubling, she needs to be nursed round the clock, my wife is grieving. Please just give me a few more days, by that time the old woman will be in Valhalla with Siegfried and Otto Klemperer, and then I shall be free to do what you ask. In the meantime I beg of you not to kill Kupki and Ludmilla, they are innocent bystanders to the ebb and flow of life. Better yet, why don't you ask Kupki to do this job, he is a much better shot than I am, it is his hobby, random killing, he will be delighted to add another notch to his belt," but Wozzeck could see the man was growing impatient, he was not paying attention to his excuses.

"Do it before the end of the week, Wozzeck, or else." And as he did not specify the nature of this alternative, Wozzeck allowed his imagination to play twenty-four bars and he could see very well what this "or else" was all about, he could not betray his friends.

"No, no, this week would not be convenient, I shall be all tied up, I am giving piano lessons to the head of Scotland Yard, if I am not there he will become suspicious and angry, especially as he wishes to learn bebop the natural way."

"This guy is sick," said the driver of the Rolls, and Wozzeck thought it the most perceptive observation of the decade, he *was* sick, sick to death of the whole damn thing, "Yes," he said, "okay, *d'accord*, I will do it before the end of the week."

"And then you will ring us, understand? Let's go through it once more."

"I dial that number you gave me, let it ring three times and then hang up, dial again, ring once and then hang up for good. Then I go home and hang myself from the toilet chain."

"What you do afterward is your own business, Wozzeck. That does not concern us, not as long as you remember to aim between the man's eyes."

He went home and listened to some music on his Walkman, and watched Heidi paint her toenails, it was what she always did when she was nervous about something, she was the Picasso of the lowest extremities.

They listened to the radio, to a concert on Radio 3, and never before had Mozart sounded so beautiful, he wanted to cry. Then they listened to a play on Radio 4, about another unhappy housewife who suffered from having too many children and too many parties to attend, and Wozzeck wanted to run down to Broadcasting House and throttle the lady, she did not know what troubles there were in the world.

At five-thirty Heidi began to cook dinner, partly out of habit, she did not wish to eat either, and partly to ensure that her mama was fed and would not make a scene and complain that Heidi was a wicked daughter, and that she wanted to die in peace, etc. The smell of it turned Wozzeck's stomach, he sat on the edge of his bed and vomited on his sneakers, and then afterward snorted another large portion of speed, he did not care that he was on a collision course with the demon Overdose.

"Yes," he said when Heidi came in to see how he was, "I am going to get it over with," there was no earthly reason for him to debate the rights and wrongs of his decision, there were no longer rights and wrongs, just the mute implacability of no longer having any choice. Heidi kissed and embraced him, whatever happened he was still her husband, the man she loved best in the world, and then suddenly he was on his way to kill a man in Hampstead, Ian Graham who had once been a baby in swaddling clothes loved by one and all, and then a slightly larger Ian Graham getting into scraps on the playing fields of Eton, Ian Graham a young man with pimples falling in love with some girl and playing interminable games of cricket, Ian Graham at university and getting married, Ian Graham entangled with the men in gray suits and dark glasses, Wozzeck could envision the man's entire life, and he felt pity for the man, for not only could he see in a flash the whole of the man's short span on earth, he would be the one to bring it to an end, and something told him this was not for him to do, the world had gone mad.

He got as far as the Archway tube station and decided to telephone ahead, just to make sure Ian Graham was in, it was a precaution that could save him an unnecessary trip. So he went into a phone booth and leafed through the directory, it was filthy, the pages were covered with all manner of unspeakable things, a forensic scientist could have had a field day with it, and there were names and numbers scribbled all over the booth, Laura the Amazon 243-5675, French Lessons ring Toni 435-9187, Irish Enemas by Eileen 877-6479, and so on, it took ages for Wozzeck to find Ian Graham, he was tempted to add his name to the surroundings, Polish Murders by Jerzy, "Hello?" said Ian Graham.

* * *

Wozzeck did not know what to say, even though he had intended to tell the man he was about to be murdered and that he should run for his life, preferably to some distant land, Tierra del Fuego would be ideal. And so he hung up and took the tube to Hampstead, the hour of Ian Graham's death was swiftly approaching.

It was when he stepped out onto the High Street that he saw his victim crossing the road. Wozzeck crossed the road, likewise, and followed the man to a restaurant on one of the side streets. It was an expensive restaurant, people were sitting on the terrace, in the heat of the evening, hee-hawing and braying and twirling linguini on their spoons and slopping expensive Chianti into their mouths, little did they know what evil was lurking in the heart of N.W.3.

Ian Graham was by himself, which was a definite advantage, and so was Wozzeck, which was also good as Heidi sickened at the sight of blood and besides did not much care for Italian cuisine. Wozzeck was reminded, as he was led to a table very near Ian Graham's, of the scene in *The Godfather* in which Al Pacino goes into the toilet and finds the gun and then comes out and shoots the antipasto out of Sterling Hayden's throat, "Then just drop the gun on the floor and walk out," Al Pacino had been instructed by the great fat mobster, "and no one will be any the wiser," or words to that effect, and although Wozzeck knew that he could have blown the man's head apart he knew also that were he to drop his gun and walk out, the world over would know he had done it, people would look at the corpse and say, "Ah, this is Jerzy Wozzeck's work," and there would be a lynch mob and a posse and he would get no farther than Mr. Mistry's newspaper shop across the street.

Wozzeck ordered a plate of spaghetti bolognese and a glass of wine and then took his time over a cigarette to case the joint out. He was confirmed in his thinking that murder in this trattoria was perhaps not such a good idea, there were witnesses everywhere, and although it would be a dramatic event in the lives of the people of Hampstead, though it would provide a subject for conversation for eons to come, he knew also that afterward he would end up precisely where he had been before, i.e., in a long dark tunnel without a light at the end of it.

He watched Ian Graham eat his dinner, he had a view of the side of his head, and while he watched him and waited for his own meal and inevitably lost his appetite for food, he fingered the pistol in his jacket pocket and knew that after Ian Graham had put down his fork and finished his wine and paid his bill he would have to follow Ian Graham, take out his pistol, and put a hole between his eyes. Of course he could never have done it here, in this restaurant, not only because they were surrounded by witnesses but also because it would have been difficult, if not impossible, to place the bullet between Ian Graham's eyes from this angle, the best he could do would be to put a hole in his ear, or just above it, or perhaps even blow off his nose—*bouf!* what a surprise that would be! Of course he could calmly rise from his chair, walk past his victim, turn the gun on him, and shoot the man's head off, but what was to guarantee that the man would sit still, "Excuse me, monsieur, but could you just sit still for a moment, I should like to put a bullet between your eyes," this would not go over very well, he could see that, not before dessert.

Now, Wozzeck was in for a shock, a big one, when Ian Graham suddenly swung around in his seat and stared at him, Jerzy wanted to disappear. The waiter poured Wozzeck another glass of wine and he drank it, calmly as you please, and smiled at Ian Graham, and tried to think of an English phrase that would fit the moment, "Hallo, cock, got a match?" or "Oi, mate, give us a kiss," they all sounded alike to him, and instead he nodded and returned to his Valpolicella as if Ian Graham were nothing in the world to him, nobody at all.

"Hallo," said Ian Graham, however, "we seem to be ending up in the same places lately," and he was smiling and speaking his best French, he had stars in his eyes, he liked perhaps the looks of Wozzeck.

"*Oui*," said Wozzeck, "it is funny, no?"

"Care to join me?"

"Ahh … *Non, merci, pas ce soir.*"

"I insist. Waiter! Kindly set a place for this gentleman here, he will be joining me for dinner."

"No, no, that is most kind of you," he did not wish to get involved, not with the man he was going to murder that night. But of course people were watching them and Wozzeck did not want to end up a tiny seed in their memories, "You recall the man who was sitting with Mr. Graham?" the police would ask them, and of course they would remember him very well, this small scruffy man in leather jacket and jeans and sneakers, they could pick him out of a crowd of two million in Red Square on May Day, "He was the one who gave Mr. Graham an argument," they would say, "the small scruffy chap, the murderer."

"You were in my shop this morning," Graham said, once Wozzeck was seated across from him.

"Yes, a beautiful place, your shop, you have exquisite objects there," even though he wanted to query the man closely as to why something as commonplace in Warsaw as a spoon was going for three hundred quid.

"A hobby, really, the antiques. I mostly do a great deal of private investing, I have other interests."

Wozzeck thought about taking out his pistol and shooting the man from beneath the table, a discreet little murder, but of course he would then not have been able to hit the man between the eyes, between the legs, perhaps, that would have been a great big surprise for Ian Graham.

"And you?" asked Graham.

"Ah. I do this and that."

"I've seen you before, you know. Now, don't tell me ..."

"In your shop, this morning," said Wozzeck, he had gone ahead and spoiled the man's little game.

"No, no, before that. In a magazine, perhaps. You're in the music business?"

"Yes, yes, that is it, I am a musician."

"Or perhaps in films?"

"Yes, yes, I am in films too, music is my hobby," he did not know what he was saying, soon he would admit to being also a pork butcher and a blacksmith and a KGB officer and the head of the mineworkers union, he would say yes to anything, that is why he was about to murder a man named Ian Graham.

"I thought so, I was sure I'd seen your face somewhere before. But you're not French, are you?"

"No, no. Polish."

"Ah. So. How interesting." Ian Graham's face was bright red, he was smiling and smoking a cigar, already Wozzeck was having mixed feelings about him.

"You're making a film here in Britain?"

"Ah, no, not at the moment," and he quickly tuned up his imagination and hoped he would be convincing as a filmmaker, he wanted to put his cap on backward and shout "Cut!" and get the hell out of it, the sweat was running into his pasta. "We are in the discussion stages of it," he imagined it was what film people said, it was a euphemism for "We are sitting on our bums doing nothing but hoping against hope."

"How very interesting indeed," Wozzeck heard him say, and although this was what the man said, word for word, Wozzeck was not deaf, he could also see a tide of suspicion rising up in Graham's eye, he did not like the feel of the undertow. "And tell me," Ian Graham went on, "what's your next project, what's in the the works? Let me rephrase that: what is the subject of your discussion?"

Now Wozzeck felt he had grounds to murder this man, funny how a turn of phrase can so offend the human ear. "Ah," said Wozzeck.

"Of course, if it's still under discussion ..."

"No, no, it is about this man, you see, and he takes a tube train to Hampstead, what a coincidence, ha-ha!, and he disappears. It's based on the novel *The Devil Wears a Figleaf*, you know it, no, of course you don't."

Graham poured Wozzeck another glass of wine and sucked on his cigar. "Tell me more about it, I'm really awfully keen on the movies, you know."

The wine was going right to Wozzeck's head, he was distracted, he said, "Now everyone thinks this guy is dead, you see, this guy who was on the tube, his wife and his mistress and his boss and his friends—"

"And his sisters and his cousins and his aunts …"

"Ha-ha-ha!" laughed Wozzeck, he could not see the joke, but he could clearly perceive a target forming between the man's eyes, "and instead he is not dead, this guy, he has been recruited by his mistress's husband to kill a man he has never met," Wozzeck did not know what he was saying, he was getting the plots confused, Ian Graham was eating it all up along with his cannelloni.

"So you'll be shooting on location, I suppose, here in London, in Hampstead perhaps?" and of course Wozzeck could only agree.

* * *

Now Wozzeck was really feeling like a character in a *policier*, Ian Graham had bought him dinner and had invited him for a stroll in Hampstead Heath, and Wozzeck the murderer and filmmaker was busy scouting out a location for his shot, someplace secluded where nobody would see Ian Graham die at the hands of an unemployed jazz pianist.

"You know," said Graham, "it's a funny thing, the plot of the film you're going to make. A couple of years ago I did some business with some men, I won't bore you with the details. Naturally I didn't know exactly what I was getting into at the time, but I made a tidy sum out of it and was able to buy a half-interest in the shop on Bond Street. But it seems these chaps think I somehow betrayed them. That's why I was a little uneasy when I saw you here after seeing you at the shop this morning. I thought you might be working for them, you see."

They stood and stared at each other, Wozzeck hiding behind his shades and grinning, there were smiles galore, even he began to laugh.

"Well of course I can see you're not working for these men. But I tell you, I've had more than my fair share of the frights lately."

They sat side by side on a bench, there were thick shrubs behind them, not a person in sight. Wozzeck wrapped his hand around the pistol, and was starting to ease it out of his pocket when he realized that once it was out in the open there was no going back, one cannot excuse a pistol in one's hand, even the normally polite English, who usually minded their own business, would have paused for reflection.

Ian Graham asked him further questions on the film business, pressed him for gossip about such luminaries as Roman Polanski and Rita Hayworth and Meryl Streep and Jeremy Irons and people Jerzy had never even heard of, and of course he had to continue to pretend he was an important Polish émigré filmmaker, and he spoke intimately about Andrzej Wajda and his old pal Roman and dear old Rita and lovely, vivacious Meryl, and Jeremy, who was such a riot, especially when he wasn't pining after unbalanced women in seaside resorts, and all the others, Wozzeck knew them all, Marlon and Jimmy and Diane and Woody, and "next week I am flying to the coast, you know, to L.A., I have meetings to attend with some studio magnates," he did not know what he was saying, but Ian Graham was gobbling away at it, and then suddenly he was suggesting that Wozzeck come to his apartment for a drink, and Wozzeck knew that zero hour had arrived, their eyes met, *I am your murderer,* said Wozzeck's look.

* * *

Now in the split second as their eyes met, it occurred to Wozzeck that perhaps he had been tricked once again. The man in the gray suit had told him that Ian Graham had betrayed UniRex and must be killed. But Wozzeck also knew that the man in the gray suit, like all men in gray suits, had a tendency to lie through his teeth, and the unhappy idea struck him that perhaps this Ian Graham was not some bit player standing in the wings of Wozzeck's tragic predicament but rather a killer of the highest caliber, like the monster in *Alien*, who after he graduated from John Hurt's stomach and grew up to be a big monster, struck fast and with uncanny accuracy, especially when you were not looking and instead messing around with a screwdriver in the bowels of your spaceship. And so as they mounted the stairs to Graham's apartment he put his hand on his gun and prayed that this was so, that Graham was in reality a hit man, because then he would have to fire in self-defense, which would let him off the hook for eternity.

The apartment resembled Ian Graham's antiques shop on Bond Street, except that none of the furnishings or *bibelots* carried discreet little price tags. There was an expensive stereo system, a table with all manner of drink on it, shelves of books, and Wozzeck listened as his victim gave him a guided tour of the place, it was like a museum, and all along Wozzeck was coming to the very substantial realization that he would have to go through with it, that Ian Graham was not a hit man, and that if he didn't go through with it there would be a massacre in Brittany, he would kick Kupki but good for the trouble he was putting him through.

"You like music?" asked Ian Graham, and of course Wozzeck could not keep his mouth shut, he spoke of his passion for jazz, and because Graham did not have any jazz records he turned on the radio to the Prom, it was Abbado conducting a big band. "Would you like to sit down?" the soon-to-be-dead man said, and he offered Wozzeck a drink, anything he liked, Wozzeck greedily swallowed great mouthfuls of vodka, it was like a scene from Dostoevsky, crime, punishment, the whole bloody circus, freaks and all.

Ian Graham sat across from him in an expensive armchair, soon there would be blood all over it, blood and brains, it seemed such a shame, for the man was talking about going on holiday soon, meaning he would be fleeing from Death, and now Death had arrived, he could not take his eyes off of Him, it was Sordid City and not a mop in sight.

Wozzeck continued to play the filmmaker, he spoke of Cannes, about the topless starlets who romped in the polluted waves, and how Burt once bought him a whiskey sour and how Clint once beat him at five-card stud, and all about Isabelle Huppert and her freckles and Gérard Depardieu's tremendous forearms, it was one of his greatest solos, the man was entranced. "And, you know, right now I am considering how to cast *The Devil Wears a Figleaf*, we have already approached many great stars of the British stage, Olivier is almost definitely with us, he will repeat his performance as a Nazi dentist, it will be most amusing, except that he won't be a dentist, he will be a Nazi chiropodist, he will do terrible things to the hero's toes."

The man continued to believe Wozzeck, he believed him because he spoke French and was from Poland, he could have talked of casting Babar the Elephant as the private detective and still the man would have believed him, he was in the palm of Wozzeck's small hand. "This film is awfully intriguing," Ian Graham said. "I told you about what happened to me a few years ago, about my little entanglement with those men. I still find it hard to believe, you know, that people can act that way. They actually threatened me. Surely you must have researched the criminal mind in preparation for your film?"

Wozzeck finished his vodka and lit a cigarette, he crossed his legs and looked interested, he was going at two hundred and seventy miles an hour, the speed was racing against the vodka, he said, "Tell me about these men, perhaps I can get a few more ideas for my project."

The man spoke of UniRex and the men in gray suits and dark glasses, he spoke too of how he had been approached by other men from another corporation, a mob he called it, he spoke of his poverty at that time, his enormous debts and alimony payments, about how his first business venture had gone straight down the drain, how he wanted to recoup his losses by writing a novel, like Jeffrey Archer, but that he couldn't get past chapter one. "So an old friend from university referred me to these UniRex chaps. One thing led to another, you see, and I found myself caught up in a real mess."

"So now you are out of it, yes?"

"I certainly hope so. There've been some telephone calls recently, anonymous calls, you know, but I haven't taken them seriously. I can't imagine anyone actually wanting to take the trouble to kill me."

Wozzeck nodded, he was suddenly not feeling very well, he nodded his head and shut his eyelids, he could not find the words to express the nothingness inside him, a murderer is eloquent only in his deed. Someone was playing a piano concerto by Beethoven, there was a great round of applause even though Wozzeck, who had been half listening to the pianist's technique, detected many naughty slips of the finger, if it had been him he would have been drummed out of the Albert Hall and buried alive in Hyde Park, he stared at Ian Graham, and suddenly Ian Graham was not quite himself, he began to tremble and fidget, he had sniffed out the odor of Death.

"You seem like a nice man," said Wozzeck. "You dress well, you have a nice apartment. I think you are also an intelligent man and, besides, you were generous enough to buy me dinner. I am making sense, yes?'

Ian Graham said yes, he shivered.

"You have a toilet here?" asked Wozzeck, the man indicated a little room between the living room and the bedroom, a little mahogany and brass room that was worth more than all of Wozzeck's residences since his birth. Wozzeck threw up and then took another hefty snort of speed, little lights were dancing around his head and his heart was pounding, and he wished to God it were he and not Ian Graham who was going to die. Even after he took his speed, though, he did not feel that much speedier, these days it came in small waves, unexpectedly, although he did not dare give up the drug. How easy it was now to take the crystal, how much an indispensable part of his life it had become, like eating and sleeping and a tune by Monk, "Straight No Chaser," for instance, how little he thought about it. Just a little nudge inside him, an echo of the old pain, and he knew it was time for a sniff-sniff.

He leaned against the washbasin and looked into the mirror and turned his eyes away, "I threw up," he told the dead man as he returned to the living room.

"Oh dear."

"I made a mess."

"That doesn't matter."

"I have come to kill you."

"Yes. It just dawned on me."

It was a lie, for Wozzeck knew that the man had grasped the truth twelve minutes earlier, Ian Graham had glimpsed it in his eyes, even though his murderer was wearing his mirrored shades and therefore all Ian Graham could see was a panorama of his own fears passing across the lenses.

"I don't want to kill you," said Jerzy, immediately regretting it because it gave the man a momentary feeling of hope, and so he added, "I don't want to kill you, but if I don't they will kill my friends and my wife and also me, I should think, what is the man on the radio going on about?"

"It's an interval talk, Christopher Ricks discussing Norman Mailer."

"And then there will be music?"

"Yes. A Rossini overture and then Britten's *Variations on a Theme of Frank Bridge.* Funny, you know. I was hoping to attend the concert tonight. Couldn't get a ticket, though."

"I would have killed you tomorrow, then," Wozzeck did not know what he was saying, he was like Bogart in that film about the gangsters and the hurricane, he was terrifying Ian Graham, it was the performance of his life.

"The UniRex people sent you, I suppose."

"That's right," said Wozzeck, cool as can be. "You were lucky, Ian Graham, you got out of it. I was not so fortunate, ah, my apologies, you didn't get out of it, actually, that is why I am here tonight."

"Perhaps we could come to some sort of an arrangement," said Ian Graham, he was shaking, there were tears.

"I must blow your brains out with my pistol and then dial a number and then I will be free to go back to Paris with my wife and her mother. They will come and look at your body and then they will let me go."

"Look," said Ian Graham, he was petrified, he hadn't moved a muscle, his eye was twitching, "why not be reasonable about this. I have money. I can give you five thousand straight away and another five tomorrow—"

"But you cannot give me yourself with a hole in your head, that is what I need to be free, you don't seem to understand that."

"Yes, yes, I see it, I really do."

"You shouldn't have got mixed up with UniRex, *mon ami.*" He put his head back and shut his eyes and watched shooting stars passing through the void and leaving no trace at all, I have overdosed, he thought, please let me die first. "I don't want to kill you," he said, "I have never killed anyone before. Have you?"

"No, I don't think so. When I was a boy I once killed a frog, it was frightfully wrong of me, perhaps we could talk this over."

"It is half-past nine, time is running out."

The man continued to tremble, tears were staining his silk tie, he said, "Look, go back and tell your people I am very sorry I spoke to their competitors. I'm just an antiques dealer, what do I know about crime, please don't kill me, I beg of you."

"You have never committed a crime in your life, Monsieur Graham?"

"Oh, damn it all, sometimes I overcharge people on the things I sell in the shop, what does it matter. Look at you—"

"Just remain seated, monsieur."

"Look at you, I'm sure you're an honest man, I'd bet you'd never been a criminal before."

"Not until now," said Wozzeck, and all at once he realized he was enjoying himself, he was in control, someone else was under his sway, body and soul, he was playing God. And he saw then the secret of the modern world, he saw too the great lie of history, the great fallacy of power struggles and war and arms races and the like, he saw how it didn't matter one bit, that in the end we are all equal, jazz musician and antiques dealer, that power was an artificial thing, it was made of steel and loaded with a cartridge, it knocked on doors and interrupted your dinner; and he saw that both of them, Wozzeck and Ian Graham, were the victims of centuries of deceit.

The audience in the Albert Hall had grown quiet and Wozzeck asked, "You have had a good life, I hope?"

"Yes," said the man, he was out of focus, tears were dripping onto his lap and his soft leather shoes with their silly little tassels, he was out of focus because Wozzeck too was crying, "yes," repeated Graham, "I suppose I have. Of course my marriage didn't work out the way I'd hoped it would. But I get to see my children once a month. Those are their pictures there, on the table. I beg of you, it is not right to kill a man with children."

Wozzeck gazed at the two girls and knew that he would never be able to kill this man, and yet were he to fail Kupki and Ludmilla would die, as would Heidi and her mama and himself, "And you," the man was asking, "have you had a good life?"

"Yes," said Wozzeck, shaking his head sadly, "it has been a ball."

The man could see Wozzeck's hand in his pocket, he could only guess at what wickedness lay within it, the drumrolls had begun, the overture to Rossini's *The Thieving Magpie* was about to go into full swing, and Wozzeck could see that this did not matter much anymore to Ian Graham, just like sixty years of jazz bore no further meaning for Wozzeck, and suddenly the music was very loud, and he took out his pistol and raised it in front of him and it struck him as very odd indeed that although he hadn't had the slightest intention of killing this poor unhappy man, that he was about to turn the weapon upon himself, and turn it gladly, the man clutched his chest and fell to the floor. "Monsieur?" Wozzeck called gently, and then "Monsieur!" he cried, but the man just lay there, his eyes open, staring in horror at Jerzy Wozzeck.

And Wozzeck could still seem to hear the man's voice, something had survived his body, a cultured, soothing voice speaking of the past, of his childhood and the blue curtains of the nursery, of discovering how flowers grew and hiding behind hedges, of exploring his Mummy's sewing basket and singing loudly in the summer noontime, of his two wonderful little girls, how they called him Daddy and loved to go to the funfair on the Heath, and Wozzeck could entwine with this the song of his own past, his own youth, his own discoveries, and they seemed to blend together, these voices, there was a hidden harmony there, and then it was just Wozzeck's voice that could be heard, and it spoke of regret and fear and disgust, and he could silence it only when he picked up the telephone and dialed the number belonging to the men in gray suits and dark glasses.

# 9

THERE IS SOMEONE AT THE DOOR, HE IS THINKING....

It is morning, and Wozzeck is opening his eyes. In the West, Mama was saying, in Paris, such a thing could never happen....

So it is morning and the old pain is returning, he has run out of speed. This is the crash, he thinks, and yet compared to what has happened in the past few months it is unremarkable, this crash, it matters little in the grand scheme of things. He has slept in someone else's apartment, he does not know why he did not return home to Heidi.

Mama thinks Heidi will be good for him, she will help him take charge of his life, she will get him to settle down. And Andrzej is such a bright boy, you cannot do wrong with a friend like that, this too she said to him....

He feels as if his body is wasting away. He is not sure he has deserved this, and he is wondering how much of it is his own doing. He can remember nothing, or rather he can remember everything up to a point. He can recall playing in Gino's club, and Kupki's proposition, "Listen," his friend had said.... Odd how a single word can change things, it was almost as if at that very moment he had sat down to watch a film, or read a *policier*, something both bizarre and harrowing, it had been so difficult lately to know what was real and what was not, he had seen so many films and read so many *policiers* in his life—and then of course there was the speed.... So this is the crash, he is thinking, this is where I bail out.... Yes ... it had been like watching a film, that was it, watching a film, a B picture to be sure, a *film noir*, and now it was about to come to an end, he had reached the last scene, it was time to step out into the Technicolor brilliance of reality....

Don't forget your hat and coat, Mama is saying....

And there are things he does not know, will never know. In a secluded farmhouse five miles outside the Breton village of Bubry, more specifically in the attic of a farmhouse, Ludmilla and Andrzej Kupki are sleeping, as is the man who has been keeping them captive and who is lying on the sofa downstairs. Beside him, on the floor, is a paperback *policier* entitled *The Devil Wears a Figleaf*, it makes a pleasant diversion from the tedium of his daily life. Ludmilla and Andrzej sleep on straw mattresses, and thus do not sleep very well. They look forward to daybreak, for each morning brings them hope that they'll be released. Soon they will rise, they will cook eggs and make toast and wait for the phone call which will signal their deliverance. They have become friends with their captor, he carries a gun at all times, he works for the men in gray suits and dark glasses. Among themselves they have often discussed what they will do when they are freed, for even the man with the gun is not free, he works for the men in gray suits. They are rising now.

Ludmilla will have a bath, she will soap her body and dry herself with a rough towel and then watch Andrzej have a bath. She hopes she will remain calm, she is angry with Wozzeck, she wants only to return to Paris and have Kupki's child, this is what she and her husband have decided to do. Now the phone is about to ring....

There is heavy traffic on the A4 heading into London. Most of it consists of people driving to work; some of the taxis and buses carry Americans who have flown to London to shop at Harrods and see the Royal Shakespeare Company. A silver Rolls-Royce can be seen in the midst of this metallic snarl, but you cannot clearly make out the occupants of this car because the windows are made of smoked glass. The Americans gaze down on it from their bus and speculate on who might be in it, they think it is the Queen, or the Princess of Wales or perhaps even Elton John or a movie star. The man in the gray suit is sitting in the back, watching breakfast television. The weatherman is predicting a brilliant day. The fat astrologer is saying that Gemini is in for a run of good luck, there could be a windfall. A cabinet minister defends his Prime Minister's economic policies, he says that the people must wait and be patient, they must believe in their leader body and soul, soon they will see the effects of her decisions. The headlines do not contain much bad news. No one is on strike. No one has yet been reported as murdered, though by the end of the day two bodies will have been recovered, one from the outskirts of Epping Forest and the other from an apartment in Hampstead. The BBC has decided to show that banned documentary on Northern Ireland. The pound has risen by a cent and a half. The man in the gray suit is playing Portfolio in the *Times*.

Wozzeck is in Ian Graham's brass and mahogany bathroom, he is dousing his face with cold water and trying to stop himself from shivering. He thinks the speed the man in gray gave him was tainted, not to mention the fact that the night before he had taken three times more than he should have and washed it down with wine and vodka. He has a strong will to survive. Now, too, his memory is beginning to return to him. He reviews the events of the previous night, and as he stumbles back into the living room and falls into a chair he is unable to bring himself to look at the remains of Ian Graham, but cannot take his eyes off the blood-spattered photographs of his two pretty daughters....

Yes, yes, now it is all coming back to him.... He recalls the meal he had the evening before. He remembers ascending the stairs with Ian Graham and listening to part of a concert on the stereo. He remembers hearing the Rossini overture *La Gazza Ladra*, *The Thieving Magpie*, he remembers taking out his pistol, he remembers that he was about to shoot himself when Ian Graham fell to the floor....

In the West, Mama was saying, there you will find the peace your papa never had....

Now Wozzeck is very puzzled indeed. He woke up with a pistol in his hand; Ian Graham had been shot in the head, there is blood and some glutinous gray substance on the wall. Now he knows for certain he has killed a man, an innocent man to boot, a man like himself, who had been victimized by the men in gray suits and shades, he has shot his brother and he might as well have shot himself. His future lies before him, he thinks, with a hole right between its eyes.

Yet this contradicts his memory. Could he have killed Ian Graham after all? But he knows this is impossible, that he could never in a million years shoot another person, he is just like his papa, he would never hurt a soul. It was bad enough that the man was frightened to death. And yet somehow the man had been shot. So one way or another the deal has been concluded. Wozzeck knows now that he and Heidi are free to return to Paris. He knows too that Ludmilla and Kupki will be released from their Breton farmhouse.

And yet he cannot quite get to the bottom of things.... It is as if he is walking from one office to another down the corridors of his memory, he cannot quite get a straight answer....

In Paris, Mama is saying ...

The silver Rolls-Royce is on the Finchley Road. The man in gray, who has just missed winning the daily Portfolio by two points, is smiling to himself, even though he has had only three hours of sleep. His night was a busy one. For a short time he had been in Hampstead, tying up some loose ends, and then he was on the phone to Paris, and then he'd been to Heathrow to speak to a baggage handler in his employ about getting a certain container onto the next flight to New York. He knows Wozzeck is still at the apartment, for he had seen him lying there, in a heavy and disturbed sleep, at half-past three that morning. It had taken him a few moments to see what had happened, and he was surprised that Wozzeck had not shot Ian Graham, for that had been their agreement. The pistol had been lying on the floor.

He is congratulating himself for having brought to a successful conclusion this unfinished business with Ian Graham.... And the small grain of humanity that still remains within him is also pleased, for Wozzeck's friends in France have been spared what had been intended as an exemplary death, slow and painful. The man in gray is thus pleased with both his power and his mercy, and now he is forgetting about it, for the past does not count for very much in his world. He is thinking about going to the health club for a swim and then perhaps on to the Athenaeum for a bite of lunch. Tomorrow he will fly to Frankfurt to meet his contacts there, and then back to Paris to dine with the head of the European office. On Friday he is to return to London and play squash with his friend the company director, and he will let his friend win by six points and then discuss business with him. He does not know that within the year, long after Wozzeck has stood trial for the murder of Ian Graham, UniRex will be crippled by a series of betrayals. He is not aware that he will spend the rest of his life in South America, hiding from the authorities. He will, however, attempt to establish his own export business in Bolivia, he will specialize in cocaine, he will travel often under a false identity to Miami and Los Angeles and New York, and one day he will be murdered by a competitor, and he won't like it one bit, a dose of his own medicine.

The Lunel family are still mourning the death of Rocco. In a few days they will receive a tip that Valenti was responsible for the murder. There will be a gang war in the streets of Paris, more precisely in Belleville. Much blood will be shed, and at least two innocent people will be killed as a result of a bomb placed by one of Valenti's men, which the press will blame on Arab extremists.

In eighteen months Rita will be on the streets of her beloved London. She will work the King's Cross district. She will perform fellatio on passing motorists for eight pounds a go. She will be arrested every once in a while, and each time she will be released and return to the streets. In three years she will be dead. There will have been a series of gruesome murders in London, and all the victims will have been women. The police will not reveal to the public the details of these horrible crimes, but they promise they will catch this monster.

The man in gray, whose future seems bright, picks up the telephone and dials a number, speaks for a few moments and then hangs up. He thinks of the convenience of having a telephone in the car. He switches on the television again. "What's today?" the voice says. "It's Tuesday!" And for a few minutes he watches *Play School*, he has always liked children.

Jerzy Wozzeck is in pain, it comes in waves, it affects his stomach and his head, his body is withdrawing from the drug. He thinks of all the jazz musicians who died this way, he thinks of Bird, and he wonders if it really has been worth it. Where had he gone wrong? He thinks too of the sax player Albert Ayler who was found in the East River lashed to a jukebox, and he considers himself lucky for not having got involved with the kind of people who did that sort of thing, they would never have given him half a chance. At least he is alive.... He sees all the blood and continues to puzzle over the conundrum. He wonders if he has been sleepwalking and also sleepmurdering. He does not see the half-finished glass of water by the kitchen sink. He does not know that there are no fingerprints on the glass, that the man with the umbrella had been wearing gloves. Now all he can do is wait. He does not know what he is waiting for, though he knows for certain that sooner or later he must do something. He thinks that in a few hours the old pain will be gone, for at the moment he is in no condition to go out into the street and return home.

Now he is rubbing his eyes and laughing a little, but it is laughter in a minor key, for he is laughing at himself. Funny how things are slowing down. It is almost as if he were watching a slow-motion film, or leafing through an album of snapshots, things are beginning to come under his control. I am in London, he thinks, I am in an apartment in Hampstead, and he wonders if Heidi has finished packing and if their home in Paris is still intact, if his records are still there, and his piano.... He does not really care one way or another, though, for he is happy to be alive. He will be glad to see Heidi. He will be happy whatever happens, he does not know that a police car is coming down the High Street, he does not understand the man in gray's sense of duty and mischief, he does not realize the obvious, that his own fingerprints are all over the pistol. He is not aware that in this world governed by men in gray suits, a world of profits and overheads and import quotas, of boardrooms and government offices, of deals and agreements and discreet payoffs, there can be no loose ends, there is no place for Jerzy Wozzeck; not here, not ever.

He shuts his eyes for a moment. In the West, Mama says, such a thing could never happen....

The police have parked their car outside the house on Gayton Road. They have been tipped off that the man inside is armed and dangerous. They are preparing to disarm and if necessary kill the man. A small crowd is gathering. Papa is speaking of Pavel Kott. What did Pavel do that was so funny today? Mama is laughing as she serves the *tchernina*, it is Papa's favorite dish, she loves her husband's stories. Every day he goes to work and comes back with new tales to tell. He is a good worker, he follows orders, he does not make trouble even though sometimes he sees things taking place.... But it is best not to talk about them, he minds his own business and does his job and looks away, that is the only way to ensure your safety, especially when it is the boss who has been caught in the act.

In the West, Mama is saying, such a thing is unimaginable, they are walking down corridors and listening to their heels echo on the tiled floors....

Another police car has parked across the road. Another small crowd is gathering. The people of Hampstead do not know what has happened in the apartment. Nothing much ever happens in Hampstead in August. A constable watches the window of Ian Graham's apartment; his partner enters the building and joins the other constables. One of them is standing outside the door, he is knocking, asking for Wozzeck. Who could that be, Mama asks, and at this hour? But Wozzeck has been roused, he opens his eyes, the dream is coming to an end, he has finished remembering. There is someone at the door, he is thinking, someone tapping out an old tune heard long ago, and suddenly he realizes what happened, he sees it all very clearly, Bird killed himself with drugs, it was his own choice, not the State's, and the man with the umbrella had come in during the night and shot Ian Graham before placing the gun in Wozzeck's hand. He is awake, he is alert, he is not back in Warsaw. And although he knows that his fate had been decided by the man in the gray suit back in Paris, and that he had yielded his will to this man and all the men who worked for him, he sees in a moment's inspiration the error of his ways. For in the West there was no need for him to become a slave. The discipline of jazz demands also the freedom to improvise. He does not have to answer the door, he did not have to get mixed up with UniRex, but he will answer the door because he is in the West and whatever has happened he is innocent until he is proved otherwise, this is the way things are done here, he read it once in a crime novel …

… and because he has the freedom of choice, because he has the freedom of choice he will answer the door, he will answer it and let the police in and show them the gun and tell his story, the whole bloody tale, from the time Kupki said "Listen" to the moment Ian Graham collapsed to the floor and died. He has been guilty of nothing save the inability to say No. He will point to the gun on the floor and tell the police about the warehouse and the dummy with the face painted on it. He will speak of Gino Vezzani and his henchmen. He will give detailed descriptions of all the men in gray suits who caused his addiction and compelled him to play a rôle in this *policier*. He will tell how they had surrendered their individuality for the sake of their organization, and then describe in twelve words or less Rita, the vacancy of her expression and the curves of her body. He knows for sure he did not shoot Ian Graham, for Jerzy Wozzeck serves no master. He has gained a foothold in certainty: I did not shoot the man, Heidi is waiting for me, Ludmilla and Kupki will be set free. In certainty lies freedom, surely Papa had always known that….

He is feeling better now, he has mastered his pain, he wants only to return to Paris. He takes a last regretful look at Ian Graham and wonders about his two pretty daughters. He will never forget Ian Graham. He will never forget his daughters, who will curse him to the end of their days. One day this would all be behind him. He would never again work for a man like Gino never again serve a master. He will devote his life to music: composing, improvising, creating a new life out of a waterfall of notes and mountains of chords, savoring the mystery in the poignancy of a precisely placed note, even now he can feel the key beneath his finger, not cold and unyielding like the trigger of a gun, but pliant and ivory-cool, a lingering B-flat, say, ah, just so....

The man is still knocking, he is waiting for Wozzeck, he is asking him to step out into the hallway.

"I'll just be a moment," and as he hums a tune to himself he rises and puts on his jacket and cap and walks to the door.

# About the Author

Photograph by Miriam Berkley

When a one-year trip to London turned to five, it became the catalyst for J. P. Smith's debut novel, *The Man from Marseille*, and launched a writing career that has spanned decades and genres. Since then, he's written such notable thrillers and mysteries as *The Blue Hour*, *The Discovery of Light*, and *Breathless*.

Alongside his novels, he's also written scripts for television, theater, and film, with one such screenplay placing in the international Nicholls Fellowship screenwriting competition. His latest work, *The Memory Thief*, is currently under review by producers. Smith is a regular writer for *The Nervous Breakdown* and lives with his wife in Beverly Cove, Massachusetts.

Made in the USA
Monee, IL
07 September 2026

62521439R00125